AMBITIOUS

K.M. SCOTT

AMBITIOUS

The exciting conclusion to Cash and Savannah's story that began in Ravenous!

The truth of who Cash March really is has been revealed for the whole world to see. Now he must face the consequences for his actions.

Just as he's found the woman of his dreams, his very future is threatened. Will she stand by him now that the truth is out?

All Savannah sees is another promise of happiness being cruelly stolen from her. This time, though, she can save the man she loves.

But will she take the chance of a lifetime and risk all she has for Cash?

Ambitious is a work of fiction. Names, characters, places, and events are the products of the author's imagination. Any resemblance to events, locations, or persons, living or dead, is coincidental.

2021 Copper Key Media LLC

Published in the United States

ISBN: 978-1-955335-04-1

CHAPTER ONE

ash

My first visit to the Gainesville police station feels pretty much like I expected it would. It's not crowded, and other than one guy who looks like he's been drunk for a month straight leaning against the dingy, off-white cinder block wall across from me, this is a pretty empty place.

Not that I had any sense I'd ever be sitting here in one of their jail cells waiting to get sprung from here by my lawyer. No, that's a surprise, to be honest, especially after the great day I was having with Savannah.

Fuck. She's probably so freaked out she'll never talk to me again. First she had to get over her shyness about hiring someone to escort her to her brother's wedding. Then she had to get past worrying that I didn't really care about her and was only spending time with her because it's my job. Now after all of that, she got to watch me get taken away in handcuffs by Gainesville's finest.

Not exactly the best ending to a date.

I wonder if they got Damon too. Probably. I hope he's been as diligent with hiding his money as he said he would be. He's sloppy with things, though. That was the whole point in us using cryptocurrencies—to be safe if we got caught. At least then we wouldn't be facing the slew of federal tax charges the United States government would bring down on our heads for neglecting to pay our fair share of taxes on the business.

Glancing around at my drab surroundings, I have to admit this cell is better than the ones back home. Well, not actually better since this one and the cell next to it are pretty much straight out of Mayberry, but cleaner, if not as modern as those in Tampa. My one and only visit to that city's jail happened what feels like a lifetime ago, and then I wasn't alone in my crime.

I watch Cade and Liam take turns pacing back and forth across the width of the cell while Alex stands near the door running his hands up and down the black metal bars. Next to me, Wilder slouches against the wall and looks utterly annoyed, like being tossed into this space with the rest of us pisses him off.

"My father is going to fucking have a fit," Cade says for the tenth time on one of his passes in front of me. "Local businessman Stefan March loses his mind and kills his only

son will be the headline on every news station. Fifteen year old gets yelled at to death. News at eleven."

Like with every other mention of how my uncle is going to react to our most recent misbehavior, I shake my head in doubt. "He'll be fine. It's my father who's going to lose his mind. Alex and I will be hearing about how we've ruined our lives every day from now on."

"And you know Mom is going to be sitting there shaking her head as Dad goes off on us," Alex says with a chuckle.

Cade stops in front of him and snaps, "What the fuck is so funny?"

"You are," Wilder says, practically growling his disgust. "This is the first time any of you have gotten into trouble outside of school. Fucking relax, for God's sake. Underage drinking isn't exactly the crime of the century. I'm guessing they're trying to scare the shit out of us by putting us in here, but nobody's going to jail for real."

Liam finally stops his pacing and glares at his brother. "I'm eighteen years old, you asshole. You're seventeen. These three might not get any real punishment, but I'm legally an adult, and this isn't your first dance with breaking the law. Or have you forgotten that? Did running the car through that guy's fence and tearing up his fucking yard make your memory disappear?"

Wilder shrugs like none of this means anything to him. Not the sitting in this jail cell with us. Not the getting in trouble yet again. Not what his mother and father are going to do when they get here.

To him, it must be all so common to have the cops stuff you into the back of a police car and drive you down here. I haven't said much since Cade's done most of the talking for the past half hour, but I'm secretly dreading having to face Cassian and Olivia March. Alex is right. Our mother will sit quietly as our father reads us the riot act, all the while silently shaking her head with a look of such disappointment that everything he says will fade away into nothingness and all that will be left will be the sadness in her eyes.

Sadness and disappointment.

Fucking Wilder. Who thought it was a good idea to let him drive home after Micah's party? Not that he was the only one who shouldn't have been anywhere behind the wheel, but any buzz the rest of us had vanished the second he jumped the curb and smashed through that metal fence.

And if any one of the five of us was still enjoying the night after that, when we got out and saw the front end of Kane's car all busted in with pieces of twisted, silver metal hanging from the grill, any good times ended right then and there.

"Don't worry, Liam. I'm the one who was driving. I told the cops that," Wilder says with another shrug. "If anyone is getting in trouble from this, it'll be me. They threw the rest of you in here because they think it's going to scare you straight."

Cade flashes him a look of pure anger, and as he stops next to Alex, mumbles, "It's going to make me want to pound the hell out of him any second now if he doesn't shut the fuck up."

Out of the corner of my eye, I see Wilder throw Cade the finger. Good to see tonight's adventure hasn't changed the shitty relationship those two have been cultivating this past year.

My father's voice hits my ear, sending a wave of terror through me. "Thank you, officer. We appreciate you bringing the boys here to make sure they're safe."

He sounds anything but appreciative as he bites the words out. Another man's voice echoes into the cell, my uncle Kane's. Anger hangs off every syllable as he says, "You can be assured they'll understand what they've done is wrong."

Liam looks over at me with utter fear in his eyes but says nothing. I wait to hear Stefan's voice, but there's nothing for a few seconds, and I swear I see utter relief wash over Cade's expression. Maybe he got lucky and he won't have to see his father until after he's heard it from his uncles.

A tiny smile lights up his face, and he stops to gloat in front of Wilder. "Maybe you're right. Maybe this won't be so bad. Well, for me, anyway."

The words barely make it out of his mouth when I see my father, Kane, and Stefan appear in front of the cell. Stefan's eyes are narrowed to angry slits to match his brothers'. So much for things being good for Cade.

When the cop opens the cell door, Stefan steps in and taps his son on the shoulder. "Trust me. This is going to be bad for all of you."

I GIVE MY BROTHER NEXT TO ME A SIDE-EYED GLANCE while my father and his brothers stand like statues glaring at all five of us. Deep inside me in the recesses of my brain, a memory of my grandmother telling me about when Stefan and my father were boys and were known as hellions by her neighbors replays on a loop. Our grandfather used to turn a blind eye to most of the trouble they caused. Maybe now would be a good time to mention that?

"Exactly what the hell were you thinking?" Kane says in a low voice tinged with rage.

Maybe some other time might be better.

Like we always do, all five of us cousins sit silently, adhering to our pledge to never give up a single one of us. I know Cade wants to blame all of this on Wilder, and something tells me this time even Liam would throw his brother under the bus, but we swore years ago when we were just kids that no matter what happened, we'd never do that.

By the look of anger in the eyes staring down at us at this moment, I get the feeling that pledge is about to be tested. After tonight, it might be every man for himself.

"Hey, buddy. What are you in for? Wearing white after Labor Day?" the drunk across the cell asks and then laughs way too hard at his own joke, pulling me out of my memories of my teenage self and that wild night with Alex and my cousins.

I smile and nod as Boozy the Clown continues to find his sense of humor hysterical. "Yeah, something like that."

A whiff of the alcohol he seems to have been bathing in earlier tonight hits my nose, and I shake my head to push that disgusting odor away. So much for this being nothing too bad. Now all I can smell is that guy's stench and all I can think about is how much I don't fucking want to be here all goddamned night.

Where the hell is Max?

A friend from law school, Max Sterling actually graduated from the University of Florida Levin College of Law, unlike yours truly. Top of his class, no less, so I thought of him as soon as the cops clapped the cuffs on me back in my condo parking lot.

Christ, Savannah was left standing there all by

herself. She couldn't even drive my car back to her house since I had the keys in my hand when the cops came at me.

I hang my head as the image of her calling a cab and waiting there in the dark next to my car parades through my brain. Fuck. I hate that she had to see me get hauled away, but even worse is how she was left there all alone.

"Cassian March!"

Looking up, I see the cop who was sitting at a desk on my way in. Short and round, he reminds me of the security guard at the mall when I was a kid.

"You've got a visitor," he says dismissively, as if the very idea that someone wants to talk to the likes of me sickens him.

I follow him out to the dimly lit hallway and down to a room with the door closed. He flings it open and points inside, like I don't know where to go. As I pass him to walk in where Max sits at a gray metal table, I give him a sideways glance and a tepid smile.

"Thanks."

He doesn't respond, clearly not interested in striking up a conversation, and slams the door behind me just as I clear it. Max simply shakes his head and smiles, chuckling as I pull out the metal chair and sit down across from him. He always did have a strange sense of humor.

"Cassian March, who would have thought it?" he asks, thankfully careful not to admit my supposed crime since we're undoubtedly being watched and listened to in this room.

"That I'd need your services one day? I would have thought that would be a certainty when you and I were hanging out at all those parties every weekend in our first year," I say with a smile, hoping he doesn't sense how scared shitless I feel right now.

"And look at us now."

I do just that and have to admire the suit he's wearing. Dark grey, very professional, and most likely expensive, it makes Max look just like a lawyer should. His hair is cut shorter now than it used to be, but then again, I'm sure that's not the only thing that's changed. I doubt he spends his time getting blasted every weekend like we used to, and I suspect he's probably not still hanging out with that girl who used to find him at every party, no matter where or when. We used to tease him that she must have LoJacked his car.

"How have you been, Max? You look like being an officer of the court suits you," I say with a smile.

"This job is everything I thought it would be and everything you worried it would be too. Long hours, uncooperative clients, and no social life. Other than this little speedbump, how have you been?"

"Still single, obviously. Just living the dream. Hey, I'm curious. Whatever happened to that girl who you used to see at all the parties back in the day? Any chance you two still talk?"

A slow smile spreads across his face, lighting up his dark eyes. "Every morning at breakfast. Tee and I are looking to get married next year."

"Ah, Tee." That's right. Her name was Teeny,

which for some reason was a nickname for Katrina, a perfectly good name that deserves a better shortened version than Teeny. "Well, good for you. Congratulations!"

Max thanks me and looks genuinely happy before saying, "I handled your bail, so you're free to leave. The prostitution charge is a misdemeanor, so there's nothing much to that. The running an escort service charge is a different story, though. You might need someone a bit more experienced in that area of criminal law, but at least I was able to get you out of here tonight."

"Thanks, Max. I'll send you the money for the bail tomorrow, and I'll have to figure out what I'm going to do after that. I appreciate you taking care of this for me."

He stands up, making his silver metal chair scratch across the industrial gray tile floor. "I have to admit I was a little surprised you called me. I would have figured you'd turn to your father for this. I'm sure he's got some big name attorneys down there on speed dial."

I nod and force a smile. The last thing I wanted to do tonight was use my one call to talk to Cassian March III. I have no idea how I'm going to explain any of this to him or my mother.

"Well, you know how it is."

Max has no idea how it is, though. All he's ever heard from me about my family is how great they are. None of what I told him was a lie. The March clan is great.

They're also people who've been laboring under the belief that I was attending law school, planning to graduate soon, and about to take the bar exam to become a lawyer. Now all of that is going to be exposed as a lie, so I'm not sure how great they're going to be anymore when it comes to me.

And we all thought Wilder was going to forever be the black sheep of the family. So much for that.

Baaaa.

"Let me know if you need anything else, Cash. Good luck. If there's anyone in the world who can get out of this mess, it's you," Max says with a chuckle and walks out, leaving me alone in the gray cinder block room with the ugly gray floors and old silver table and chairs.

Hell of a place jail is. Let's hope this is my last time to see it.

CHAPTER TWO

ash

I STARE AT MY FRONT DOOR, UNSURE WHAT I'LL FIND when I walk into my apartment. No doubt, the cops have rifled through every last inch of the place. Thank God I never leave my phones lying around for just anyone to search.

Not that I ever would. Between the business and Emily's tendency to be nosy, nothing was ever safe, even here at home. Those three work phones are safely in the place I always keep them when I'm not here.

The post office box I rent under the name Cash Lucas and have for the past three years. Being borderline paranoid about things has its benefits.

As I push the door open and hear that squeak that started about two months ago, I slowly peek in and hope to God the cops didn't leave the place looking like a goddamned mess. I get that they have their job to do and they had to search for any evidence of the crime they claim I've committed, but that doesn't mean they have to make it look like a hurricane roared through.

Three steps in and I see that's exactly what they did. Fuck. Every piece of paper in the place is thrown onto the tables or floor, except for those I'm sure they took with them. They found nothing since I keep not a shred of proof of anything Damon and I are up to lying around, but they probably realized I have a tendency to keep every piece of junk mail I've ever received since the day I moved in. It's an odd habit but one I've never been able to break in all the years I've lived here.

The sofa and chair cushions sit turned over on their pieces of furniture in the living room, and the coffee table in the middle of the room looks like someone dumped a year's worth of that junk mail in the center of it. Scattered on the floor around it are stray envelopes and fliers that slid off the top away from the rest of the pile.

"Thanks, guys. All of this and you found nothing since I don't even own a damn computer."

That thought makes me laugh. They probably think I'm hiding a laptop or tablet somewhere, but in the business Damon and I are in, there can be no paper trail, electronic or otherwise. Phones are a necessary evil, so those I use, but any kind of computer is the surest way to get caught, so when we started, we agreed we wouldn't use any.

Even my phone, which technically can be considered a computer, shows no online activity whatsoever. When they searched that after they brought me in tonight, they probably wondered where the fuck the social life of a twenty-four year old man exists on it since I have no social media presence at all.

In fact, all they found on my phone were my family's phone numbers and Savannah's number. And Emily's because I forgot to delete her after that last charming experience with her.

As I told Damon in the beginning, if you're going to walk on the wrong side of the law these days, you better be prepared to do it the old fashioned way. Nothing to show you live at all. As far as the online world is concerned, Cassian March IV doesn't exist.

And until those cops showed up outside my car tonight, I didn't. Now that's all changed, though. Just how much I guess I'll find out in the next few hours.

In the meantime, all I want to do is take a shower and go to bed. I think that drunk's stink still clings to me, and maybe if I can get a few hours of good sleep, I'll be able to forget about all of this for a little while.

One look into my bedroom tells me dreamland is going to have to wait. First I need to put my mattress back where it belongs and clean up the mess all over the floor, along with putting the dresser drawers back. Nothing like ransacking the place in the name of the law.

. . .

MY PHONE VIBRATING ON MY NIGHTSTAND WAKES ME up, and I look at the number to see it's Savannah. Damn, I want to talk to her, but I can't right now. I still don't know what to say to her. Sure she knew what I did for a living, but she didn't know I was lying to her about my name and that I owned the business instead of just being someone who worked as an escort.

I stare at her name and wait for the phone to stop ringing even as I quietly say into the darkness of my bedroom, "I'm sorry. I wish I could talk, but I don't know how to explain yet."

When my phone's screen goes dark, I consider trying to fall back to sleep, but that's not going to happen. Seeing Savannah's name made everything I feel about her come rushing back. There won't be any more sleep for me tonight.

So I call my brother since I'm going to have to tell someone in my family about what happened. Alex is a good starting point. He's easy going and won't freak out like my parents. I need that mellow thing he has about him right now.

When he answers, I instantly feel more relaxed. "Hey, Cash! What's up? Isn't a little late for you to be calling? Aren't you normally in bed or at the library or something?"

He stops dead and says, "Oh, yeah. That's right. You're not in school. I'm still having a hard time getting used to that."

"Funny. Time to adjust your lame jokes to this new reality. Speaking of that, I've got something else you're going to have to get used to. That's the reason I'm calling, actually. I figured you're the first person in the family I should tell."

My statement is met with silence for a long moment before Alex quietly asks, "Cash, are you getting married?"

He sounds confused and worried. I don't think I've heard that tone in his voice since we were kids.

"No. Why?"

"Because you sounded like you're about to tell me you're getting married. Well, that or you're coming out, but I'm thinking you're not suddenly gay, so engaged is what I went with."

His logic makes me laugh. "Well, I'm not engaged or gay. And why the hell are you so obsessed with my sexuality?"

"I'm not. You just sounded like you were about to confess something, so I went with that or the getting married thing."

"Well, enough with the gay business. I'm not ever going to come out since I'm straight."

"Okay. Then what are you calling to tell me?"

I take a deep breath in and let it out slowly, trying to find the right words to describe what happened last night. Best to just say it and then deal with what comes out of his mouth next. This is Alex, so it's not like he's going to freak out or anything.

"Remember that escort service I told you about. Well, I got arrested tonight, charged with a host of things, including prostitution. That's what I'm calling to tell you."

I hear Alex's sharp intake of breath followed by what I imagine is him blowing every last bit of breath from his lungs as he processes my news. I can see him sitting wherever he is, probably in his apartment, and making that face he does whenever he's thinking about something. It's always reminded me of how he looks when he's in pain, like mulling things over upsets his normally very casual and relaxed state of mind.

"Arrested? As in…"

When he doesn't continue speaking, I finish his sentence for him. "As in, they put me in handcuffs, stuck me in the back of the police car, and took me down to the police station where they threw me into a jail cell with some drunk guy who stunk like three day old gin. That kind of arrested."

"Is there another kind?" he asks, instantly easy the tension.

Leave it to my brother to say that.

"No, smart ass."

"Uh, are you using your one phone call to call me, Cash?" Alex asks, sounding distinctly worried suddenly.

Now it's my turn to laugh.

"No. I knew someone who could help me, and Max posted my bail, so I'm back home. Right now, in fact, I'm in bed, which I had to put back together after the cops searched the place and left it looking like someone robbed me. Ironic, don't you think?"

My attempt at being lighthearted about this whole thing falls flat, though.

"Cash, what's going to happen? Do they have a

case against you? What charges are you looking at? Jesus, man. This sounds serious."

So much for Alex being easy going and a good place to start with the March family.

"Well, I'm going to have to find a better attorney, first of all. Max is a great guy, but he doesn't handle criminal cases. He just did me a favor so I didn't have to spend the night propped up against the wall of a jail cell with some boozehound across from me. As for the case, I don't know yet. No matter how careful you are, sometimes things slip through the cracks. I'll have to see. I think the most embarrassing charge is the prostitution charge since I'm considered the prostitute, but there's a host of others related to running a business that run the gamut from wire fraud to tax evasion, but they're federal."

My level-headed explanation does little to make my brother sound anything less than concerned. "What about Mom and Dad? They don't know yet, do they? What are you going to say to them?"

"I have no idea," I answer truthfully.

Or almost truthfully. In fact, I do know what I want to tell them. The truth. I just don't know how I'm going to say that. I'm hoping to find a way to ease them into the reality of my being arrested for the crimes the Gainesville police say I committed while at the same time be honest about not attending law school all this time.

It's going to be a lot to take in, especially for my mother.

"Whatever you do, I think you should do it in

person. Tell them face to face, Cash. Don't do it over the phone. Remember, when it comes to Mom, she's always had a weak spot when it comes to you, so use that to your advantage. It'll make her feel better about everything. Trust me on this."

I know what he's saying is right, but damn, the last thing I want to do is have to face my mother with those sad brown eyes of hers when she hears what her little boy has been up to. As for my father, I'm almost hoping he does lose his mind. It will be better than those few times Alex or I has gotten into trouble and he shuts down, unable to say anything and simply walking around the house sighing loudly.

"Yeah, I have to figure all of that out. I think I have a little time for that, though. My first court appearance isn't for a few weeks, so by then, I'll have an idea of what's going to happen so I can be as honest as possible with them."

"Well, maybe you should focus on your entrepreneurial spirit when you talk to them. Mom and Dad love that kind of thing."

That he says those words without a hint of a chuckle stuns me. "My entrepreneurial spirit? Okay. I'll try to fit that in somewhere between the prostitution charges and the felony tax evasion issues."

"I didn't say it would be easy. Just ease them into it. It'll be a shitshow, I'm pretty sure, and I won't want to be within ten miles of that little get-together, but they're Mom and Dad, Cash."

There's the Alex we all know and love.

"Thanks for the support. I'll be sure to give you a

head's up when the shitshow meeting is on the schedule. Maybe you can take off some vacation days from the restaurant."

That makes him laugh. "Don't joke. I'm thinking I should. The last thing I want is to be around when that goes down."

As much as my brother is busting my ass about this, I'm happy he's acting this way. It gives me hope that when I do finally tell my parents and the rest of the family that they won't go nuts and lose their minds.

It is, after all, just a few charges.

"I need to get going, Alex. Keep all of this to yourself, okay? I don't want anyone to know before I tell them."

"No problem. Just don't wait too long, okay?"

"I won't. Just long enough to let everything calm down so I can get a handle on things and then I'll come down to talk to them."

"Talk to you later, then. Remember, do it in person, Cash."

Easier said than done, but I know my brother's right. I can't avoid doing this face to face. I just have to man up.

In a couple weeks or so.

After talking to Alex, I close my eyes and think about Savannah and what she's up to right now. She's probably dying to talk to me to tell me how much she hates me for what happened.

I wouldn't blame her. It's not every day a woman like her gets to see her date led off in handcuffs and put into the back of a police cruiser.

ash

My phone vibrates against the top of my nightstand, ripping me out of a great dream about Savannah and me at the beach, and I see my father's name on the screen. Unsure if I want to answer the call, I silently curse Alex for not even waiting twelve fucking hours before telling my father about what happened. It's barely morning and that jackass gave up my secret.

Some brother he is.

Swallowing hard, I work to get my courage up and answer the phone. "Hey, Dad. What's new?" I ask as casually as possible.

The next time my brother needs my help, he better go looking somewhere else.

My father doesn't say anything, so I pull the phone

out to see if maybe the call dropped. Nope. Still there. Great. He's probably getting himself mentally prepared to ream me out.

"Well, Cash, I just figured I'd call and see how things are going for you up there."

He sounds odd, like he's trying to restrain himself, but it's not like my father to beat around the bush. Maybe Alex didn't rat me out.

So I figure I'll feel the situation out for a few seconds. "Not much. You know, the same as always. Did you talk to Alex? He and I talked last night."

More silence, but I can hear my father breathing. He sounds like he just came back from a run. Maybe that's why he's not saying much. But if that's the case, why did he call me at all?

Oh my God. Something's happened with my mother!

"Dad, is anything wrong? Is Mom okay?" I ask as my hands begin to shake.

Standing up from the bed, I start to walk toward the kitchen to get a glass of orange juice when he finally tells me what's going on.

"Your mother's fine, Cash. Well, except for how she felt when she saw the segment on the morning show she watches about how you were arrested for running an escort service yesterday and are looking at prison time. Oh, and the crews from the local TV stations camped out at the end of our driveway reporting on it probably isn't helping her to feel all fine and dandy either. I guess there's really nothing as wonderful as being trapped in your home by local news crews, Cassian."

Jesus. All I can imagine is my mother sitting at the table with her morning coffee blissfully watching some show as she slowly wakes up when the news about me stuns her and she goes running through the house frantically looking for my father like her hair is on fire to tell him what happened.

Every word he says hits me like a punch to the face, and when he finally ends with the name we share, one that he only uses when he's furious with me, I know things are bad there. I open my mouth to apologize, but somehow, the words just don't come out.

"Well, I think this might be the reason you weren't thrilled about the graduation party your mother and grandmother were planning, isn't it? No need for that since you quit going to law school two years ago!" he barks into my ear.

"Dad, I can explain."

Having the ability to and actually wanting to are entirely different animals, though.

"Can you? Can you honestly tell me there's a good reason why you lied to everyone who loves and cares about you? For years? You lied to us for years."

"I know, Dad. I do."

As I start to try to explain, he interrupts me. "Years, Cash! I can't count how many times I heard your mother gush about how proud she was of you attending law school. She's been talking about this goddamned graduation party for you for at least six months, for God's sake, and not even a couple weeks ago you sat at your grandmother's house for hours while she and your mother buzzed around making plans for the cake and the caterer, while the whole time you knew damn well there could never be any party since you quit going to law school ages ago. Please, Cash, tell me how you can explain."

I let the phone fall silent for a few seconds, sure he has more to say. I deserve every word he plans to utter. Good, bad, ugly, it doesn't matter. I have them all coming to me and more.

But he doesn't say anything, so I take a deep breath and begin to tell my story. "I'm so sorry, Dad. I am. Really. I never wanted to hurt you or Mom or anyone, for that matter. I didn't. The problem was I just didn't want to be a lawyer. I thought I did, but it only took one semester here to know that wasn't the life I wanted. I knew how proud you and Mom were to have me in law school, so I didn't want to disappoint you. I never meant to lie for this long. Things just got out of hand, and after a while, I just didn't want to think about having to confess the truth to you."

None of that is a lie. What I'm carefully leaving out is how much I've enjoyed running the business and making all that money. Now doesn't seem like the time to get into that.

My father lets out a heavy sigh and groans. "Well, I guess the next thing we need to do is get you a good lawyer. I have someone in mind, if you don't have a problem with me helping out."

"Sure, Dad, but I thought you'd want to talk about the reason I got arrested," I say, honestly confused why he hasn't even touched on that part of what happened.

"When you get here, then we'll talk about that. For now, I just wanted you to know how hurt your mother and I are to find out that you've lied about being in law school all this time."

While I appreciate getting the surprise break and not having to get into the nuts and bolts of running an escort service with my father right now, I can't help but wonder why he's avoiding that subject. "I'm sorry, Dad. I'm sure the whole escort service part only makes it worse, especially for Mom."

"That's something for the legal system to deal with, so I don't want you to bring it up again today, okay, Cash? For now, let me get to finding you a lawyer, and you focus on getting back here as soon as possible."

"But won't that just make the media focus all their attention on you guys?"

I get another groan and he says, "You'd have to see the end of the driveway to know how impossible it is for the media to focus any more attention on us here. I guess maybe if foreign countries' networks start broadcasting from the street it might get bigger, but it's pretty bad already."

"I'm so sorry, Dad. Is this going to affect the restaurant? I hope they don't bother you there. Maybe if you and Mom went away for a little while until this initial excitement blows over. Take the money you were going to spend on my graduation party and put it toward a cruise or something. Anything to get away."

"Kane will handle anything that happens at the restaurant. He's surly enough that they won't bother after the first question when he slams the door in their faces," my father says with a chuckle. "As for your mother and me, we're staying put, but we expect to see you here later today. This is a time to circle the wagons for our family, Cash."

Wincing at his mention of my family, I hang my head. "Okay, Dad. I'll get my things together and come down. See you in a few hours."

"Good. I'll tell your mother you're coming."

The phone goes dead. The very idea of facing my mother with her sad, disappointed eyes fills me with dread.

As I pack up my stuff for my trip home, I can't stop myself from turning on the news. I know my father said they were being inundated by their local stations back home in Tampa, but I doubt it's actually as bad as he thinks. Damon and I are tiny fish in a huge pond, even up here, so it's probably only one station that had a report about it because the whole idea of an escort service sounds salacious. My parents probably merely feel overwhelmed because they're such private people.

I toss one of my favorite shirts into a suitcase as some story about a bobcat loose in a local elementary school begins. See? The story of our escort business getting busted doesn't even rank higher than a wild animal on the prowl feature.

"And now for our lead story, the arrest of the owners of the escort service that's been running right here in Gainesville for years, right under everyone's noses. We've got team coverage on this breaking story starting with reporter Casey Grounder outside the home of Cassian March, one of the owners of the business. Casey, what else do we know?"

My mouth drops open when I see the front of my building right there on the TV screen in front of me. So much for thinking this isn't really a big deal here.

The pretty brunette reporter with perfectly straight, white teeth flashes a grin that seems inappropriate for the big deal they're making of this story. I know I should turn off the TV, but it's like I can't stop myself from hearing them talk about my problems.

"Sheila, I'm here in front of Cassian March's apartment building where police arrested him last night here in the parking lot. He's being charged with a variety of crimes, but the most serious is running an illegal escort service focused on women exclusively."

I wait for her to flesh out that statement a little, but she stops talking and before my eyes, I see the men I've known for months, some for years, being paraded across my screen as they're led into the police station today. Over the images, the reporter begins once again to explain our horrible crimes, but this time she gives a bit more color to the two ringleaders, as she calls us, Damon and me.

"The two owners, who police are calling ringleaders of this organization, are Cassian March IV and Damon Childress. Both men attended law school at the University of Florida right here in Gainesville, but both are dropouts, records show. Their business catered exclusively to women looking for male escorts, but authorities say the truth is they preyed on unsuspecting women."

What the fuck is she talking about? Nobody was unsuspecting. The hoops we made them jump through just to find us, never mind the details we required before even considering pairing a client with one of our escorts, meant there wasn't a chance in hell any of the women could be thought of as prey for us or unsuspecting in any way.

And just when I think it can't get worse than being described as predators and seeing my employees perp walked in handcuffs into the police station downtown, the perky Casey hands over her coverage to another reporter who's standing in front of a home I recognize immediately.

Savannah's house.

"Casey, thanks. We're here in front of the home of Savannah Gardener, the widow of the wildly successful hotel mogul Carson Gardener. Mrs. Gardener is one of the women caught up in Mr. March and Mr. Childress's escort business."

My eyes grow wide in horror when I see Savannah open her door and look out at the news crew with fear. Christ, she looks mortified.

Damnit, I never wanted this. None of this was ever supposed to happen.

CHAPTER FOUR

*S*avannah

"MRS. GARDENER, THE POLICE SAY THEY'RE looking into charges for the women who hired the escort service. What do you have to say to that?" the blond reporter calls out from the street and then leans forward toward me, thrusting her microphone with her TV station's logo as far as her arm can stretch.

I don't say a word, merely shaking my head in disgust that every time I look out these vultures swoop in to ask me more questions. I want to say that this is a victimless crime. That what the escort service did for women like me was let them attend social functions without feeling like some kind of sad freak or outcast because they don't date much and finding anyone to go to weddings with is difficult in the best circumstances.

My attorney has already warned me they'd try to scare me into saying something with threats of prosecution, but I'm not worried. I did nothing wrong. If the police in this town want to humiliate women just to show how prudish they are, then they can go ahead.

I have enough money to humiliate them right back.

"Honey, just close the door!" Cheyenne yells from the living room, frustrated I insist on actually seeing what these people are up to out here.

I slam it in their faces and march back through the house to the kitchen. When my husband was alive, we often had press wanting to speak to him. He was a powerful man and a successful hotel owner, so it wasn't surprising.

They never acted like this, though. Then again, Cash isn't like him.

Cassian March IV, more correctly. That sounds far more imposing than the name Cash. No wonder they keep using it like he's some supervillain. And he lied about his last name. I guess I don't have to ask why.

So the man I fell in love with wasn't just some hired escort who ended up liking me. He's the co-owner of the service. I wish he would have told me.

Cheyenne sits down at the island in front of me and clears her throat. "You're getting lost in your head again, Savannah. Stop thinking about things. Trust me. It's not going to make them any better."

I grit my teeth so I don't snap at her again this morning and turn around to get water from the refrigerator. "I'm not getting lost in my head."

Behind me, she sighs. "You are, but it's not a bad

thing, per se. It's just that I worry you're going to get depressed when you realize everything that's happening."

I set the glass water pitcher on the counter between us and look directly into her eyes. "You mean like we're going to be shunned because we dared to only want men to have on our arms for special occasions and not every day? Or do you mean the part about my falling for a man who wasn't really an escort but a businessman the local press is making out to be some kind of Casanova law school drop out?"

My sister's eyes open wide as I say what's truly on my mind, but then a sly smile lights up her beautiful face. "I don't think I've ever heard you sound so strong, you know that?"

"Well, maybe I'm just tired of being a victim. We did nothing wrong. I think that's something worth saying and saying with some strength."

Cheyenne slides her hand over to touch mine and gives my fingers a gentle squeeze. "You really like him, don't you? For what it's worth, I think he might be good for you, Savannah."

"I do, but it might all be a moot point anyway since I can't seem to get in touch with him. I've tried three times already, but it always just goes to voicemail."

"Honey, they probably took his phone off him. That's how it always happens in the movies. They confiscate the bad guy's phone and all his laptops to find out what evidence they can glean from them to use against him."

Yanking my hand away, I pour myself a glass of

water and correct her terminology. "Cash is not a bad guy. Don't call him that."

A sheepish look settles into her expression. "I didn't mean it that way. I was just talking about what happens in movies when they bring someone in to arrest him. I'm guessing that's why you can't get in touch with him. That's all."

I push a glass of water over in front of her and try not to glare at her. "Fine, but don't call him a bad guy again. We don't know all the facts about any of this."

"We know he ran an escort service the two of us used. At least we can say we know that."

She seems to want to discuss this, but I don't. I don't care about the legality of what Cash and his partner did. Nobody got hurt. They provided a service women like us asked for, and if I hear that idiotic woman on the news call us "unsuspecting women" one more time, I'm going to scream.

My cell phone rings for the first time today, and I excitedly look to see who's calling, hoping it's Cash. It isn't, sadly. Instead, I see the one name I definitely didn't want to see this morning.

Cecile.

I hold up the phone to show Cheyenne the name. Instantly, horror fills her eyes.

"Don't answer it!" she says, practically pleading with me to not talk to our older sister right now. "You know she's going to be a nightmare about this."

Nodding, I swipe to answer it anyway. "Hello, Cecile. How are you this morning?"

And with that, I put the call on speaker and set my

phone on the countertop between Cheyenne and me. Like I suspect, it takes about two nanoseconds for our older sister to start her nonsense.

"How am I? Utterly humiliated is how I am. How could you do this, Savannah? You brought that man around our family. Our family! Have you no respect for us or yourself?"

"He wasn't infected with a communicable disease, Cecile. The man simply ran a business. Stop overreacting."

She stammers out a few unintelligible words that sound like some kind of prayer for someone to come save us all from damnation or something like that and then says, "This is so utterly embarrassing, Savannah. I had no idea you were so desperate as to hire a man to pretend to be your date. I don't know how I'm going to ever show my face again at the club."

My feelings are instantly hurt, but even more, I'm angry at her attack on me, so I don't hold back when I answer. "You mean the club where I'd bet at least some of the women have hired men from Cash's escort business? That club? Don't kid yourself, Cecile. I wasn't desperate. I simply didn't want to get involved in a relationship and this made it easy for me to attend things like Spencer's wedding so I wasn't a sitting duck who would have to tolerate all your comments about my being single."

I barely finish when Cheyenne leans forward and says into the phone, "And you can add me to the list of women who used that service too, Cecile. That guy Nico who was my date for the wedding? An escort.

And that wasn't the first time I've used them either. So get off your high horse and try living in the twenty-first century where women don't have to be married if they don't want to be."

She's so sassy, which is nothing new for my younger sister, but this time I'm right there with her. "Right. So just keep your talk of humiliation and anything else you want to say today to yourself. We're fine, so thank you for calling. Since I'm sure Mom and Spencer plan on doing the same thing you just did, tell them they don't have to. Feel free to give them the Cliffs Notes version of what we said, though. That way everyone can be up to speed."

And with that, I press END and that's the last I want to hear from my family about this matter.

Cheyenne jumps off the barstool and throws her hands up in the air. "That was the best thing ever! I never knew you could be such a badass, Savannah."

Now that all those sassy words came out of my own mouth, I have to admit I'm a little shocked. "I didn't know either, to be honest."

"I like this new you," she squeals, pointing at me like I'm something amazing. "I definitely like it."

With a heavy exhale, I let the air out of my lungs and try to calm myself. "I've never spoken to anyone like that. Cecile is probably thinking I've lost my mind. You know what? I don't care. Let her think whatever she wants."

"She's just a stick in the mud anyway, so forget her. I'm still not convinced Mom didn't have an affair with some cool mailman to have you and me because

Cecile and Spencer are the world's two biggest flat tires."

I smile like I feel as confident as she does, but I can't help but hate that our family is embarrassed by us. Why do they have to be so uptight? What crime is it to want to have someone to go to family events with like Cheyenne and I did with Nico and Cash?

"Don't worry, Savannah. I see it written all over your face. You're worried Mom and Dad are going to be angry with you. Trust me. This will all blow over. I won't let you deal with it alone, though. Nico and all those other guys I spent time with from Cash's escort service were some of the best dates I've ever had. They wanted me to be happy, and I got exactly what I wanted. Plus, that Nico was an okay guy and a fantastic lay."

My mouth drops open in shock. "You slept with him?"

Cheyenne tilts her chin up proudly. "Of course, I did. You saw him. I would have been crazy not to. He's gorgeous with a body to die for. It was the best part of the day, and I regret nothing."

I burst out in nervous laughter at my sister's admission. If only I could be as badass as she is. "He really was gorgeous. Good for you. I'm glad you had a good time. Too bad the poor guy was arrested."

"For making women happy! Leave it to this place to be so damn provincial," she says before sitting down on her barstool again. "What kind of world is it we live in when putting a smile on a woman's face is a crime? Seriously, you'd swear the guy was a serial killer or something. It's ridiculous. The cops should be spending their time on real crimes and leave guys like Nico and Cash alone."

None of what she says is wrong, but I know the world doesn't work like we want it to. I don't like it, but that's the way it is.

"And another thing," Cheyenne says, clearly not done with her rant. "If they have the nerve to come here and arrest me for sleeping with a man, you better believe I'm not going without a fight. I'll be like those suffragettes from the nineteen-hundreds. They'll have to carry me out kicking and screaming. Give me liberty and a hot guy or give me death!"

I roll my eyes at her historical mistake. "That wasn't the suffragettes who said that. That was Patrick Henry from Revolutionary War times, and I'm pretty sure he never included the hot guy part."

Cheyenne waves away my correction. "Whatever. It's the same idea. Just giving you fair warning. I'll make them drag me out of here, a man on each limb with me telling them how wrong it is the whole time. They can take away our men, but they can't take our freedom!" she yells, pushing her right fist high in the air.

The image of Cheyenne creating a scene that would make my sister and mother die of embarrassment flashes through my mind, and I can't help but laugh. "Nice. Braveheart references. I'm sure William Wallace would relate to our plight."

"I'm not kidding. I'll do it."

"Well, at least that will take the attention off of me.

Right now, I'm the worse of the two of us since I was with the guy who was the owner of the escort service. You just went out with one of his guys. In the ranking of mistakes, mine's far graver."

My sister's sags against the island and sighs as a frown makes the glee in her face from a moment ago drain away. "I'm sorry about getting you involved in all of this. I was just trying to help. I hope you know that."

I take her hand and give it a sympathetic squeeze. "Don't feel like you have to apologize. I'm happy I got involved with Cash and his business. I don't regret a thing, just like you. And if we're being honest, I slept with him and I don't regret a second of that, to be sure."

A smile brightens Cheyenne's face. "Good. I am sorry for giving you such a hard time about him, though. That was wrong. You were happy, and I was being an overprotective bitch. I'm sorry, Savannah."

"No apologies needed. You worry about me. That's a good thing. He's a good guy, though. Honest. I mean, other than the whole getting arrested thing. He makes me smile and he makes me remember what being twenty-seven feels like again."

We fall into silence as the sounds of horns outside remind me the madness of what's happened is mere yards away, no matter how much I wish it wasn't. If only Cash would call me and let me know he's okay. I'd understand if he couldn't see me because of the trouble he's in, but at least I'd be able to let him know I don't hate him for lying to me.

"You know what?" Cheyenne says, interrupting my thoughts about Cash.

Shaking my head, I smile. "No, what? You plan on laying siege to the news trucks outside?"

"Don't give me any ideas, but no. I was just going to say that I think Carson would like it that you found someone to make you happy."

My chest tightens at the mention of my husband and what the press is probably going to do to his name and his memory with all of this. "You think he'd be okay with me being tied to an illegal escort service and having those people outside dying to hear all the scandalous details of my time with Cash?"

My sister screws her face into a scowl. "Are you done glossing over the dirty life your husband led before and during the time he was married to you? Because everyone who isn't living in a dream world remembers. Carson was a great guy, but he was a cutthroat businessman who would eat weak people for lunch. I bet he'd be impressed with Cash and his idea of starting a business catering to single women looking for dates and romance and no commitment. I bet he'd pat him on the back and congratulate him for seeing a need and filling it."

"No pun intended?" I say, barely able to control my giggles.

She rolls her eyes at my attempt to change the subject. "Maybe I intended that pun. Whatever. All I'm saying is Carson was a savvy businessman who didn't always walk on the right side of the law, if I remember correctly. I'm thinking of that time when he was dealing with the Brazilian government and things required a little monetary persuasion, as he called it when he told us the story. That was a bribe, Savannah, and Carson wasn't above doing that because he wanted that hotel to open, come hell or high water. I think you might just have a type, big sister. You go for the charming and debonair businessman who's actually a criminal on the side."

I wave away that absurd suggestion, but I have to admit both Carson and Cash do have one thing in common. Both of them had a way of making me feel like the most beautiful woman in the world and both made me feel like I was the most important person to them.

And just like with Carson, Cash made me fall in love with him, even though I didn't think it could be possible to love again.

Maybe I do have a type after all.

CHAPTER FIVE

ash

THE CROWD OF REPORTERS AND SPECTATORS ON THE street outside my parents' house make it impossible to get into the driveway. They rush toward the car, banging on the hood and the windows like crazy people, and I blast the horn to try and scare them away.

It doesn't work. They just scream louder and hit the windows harder with their fists. What the fuck is wrong with these people?

I punch the steering wheel, repeatedly honking the horn as I try to move the car forward. I get only a few inches toward the driveway when someone bangs so hard on my window that I'm sure they're going to punch their fist through the glass.

Pressing the button to lower it, I scream, "Move

out of the way! If you don't, I'm going to run you over!"

My words barely register with the man trying to climb in through my driver's side window, much less the rest of these people. I keep pressing on the horn and inching the car forward as I pray to God no one actually gets hurt since I don't need a charge of vehicular homicide added to the list of charges I'm already facing.

"Cassian March, are the accusations true?" someone screams at me from just outside the window. "Are you a pimp?" another person yells.

A woman who reminds me of the perfect smile reporter from Gainesville sticks a cell phone into the car close to my head and asks, "Were you running a prostitution ring? What about all those women you took advantage of?"

I want to scream fuck off as an answer to every question, but I somehow find the patience and strength to ignore every word as I continue to crawl toward my parents' driveway. If I can only get onto their property, this will all end.

At least for now.

Just as I'm about to cross over the sidewalk and finally get away from these insane people, a woman yells, "Reports are that the Gainesville police are considering charges against Savannah Gardener. Do you have any comment?"

My heart sinks at the thought that Savannah would be caught up in all of this. I want to lash out. I want to run down all these assholes who get such joy from dragging an innocent woman into my mess.

I shake my head and step on the gas to drive away toward the house. Thankfully, none of the crowd gets in front of the car and I don't run anyone over, even though at this moment nothing would make me happier.

By the time I reach the house, I feel like someone's been beating me with a club for the last twenty minutes. I turn off the car and close my eyes, resting my forehead against the steering wheel and wishing I could push all of the madness away while I think about Savannah.

I have to call her. Even if she hates me, I have to at least try to make her see what we had was real. I didn't sleep with her because it was my job or part of the business. I care for her. She has to know that, at least.

A tapping on my window startles me out of my thoughts, and I turn to see my father standing outside the car. He looks like the personification of disappointment. Even his blue eyes, which always appear so bright and alert, seem dimmed as I look at him now.

The second I open my door, I hear the crowd screaming at the end of the driveway. I look away, unable to deal with seeing their nearly rabid-looking faces as they yelp and shout up at me.

"Hi, Dad," I say as I slam the door.

"Best to bring in whatever bags you have now. I don't think this nonsense is going to subside any time soon today," he says with a tiny smile that looks like it's painful.

I nod and grab my suitcase out of the trunk. With one last glance at the throng of people still yelling questions at me, I shake my head and walk into the house. The sooner all of them just go away, the better life will be for everyone here.

Especially my parents.

My mother sits in the living room watching TV, but the sound is down so low that all she must be able to hear is the racket from outside. She doesn't acknowledge me when I enter the room, but I know I can't avoid her and her eyes full of sadness and disappointment for another moment.

Sitting down across from her, I take a deep breath in and paste a smile on my face. "Hi, Mom. What are you watching?"

Only her eyes move to glance over at me and then she returns her focus to the TV. "I don't know. Nothing, I guess."

She looks the same as always with her red hair pulled back into a bun, but something's very different today. Not that I can't put my finger on exactly what that is. I fucked up, but even more, I lied to her about something that was probably one of the most important things in her life.

A little small talk isn't going to cut it this time.

"Mom, I'm sorry about all of this. The people outside, the media, everything. I never wanted you and Dad to have to deal with anything because of me."

She doesn't turn her head to look at me or even

glance over now. I get nothing—no anger, no sadness, no reaction at all. My mother simply stares straight ahead toward the TV perched above the fireplace.

"Cash, let's go into my office and talk," my father says, breaking the silence that's descended over this room.

"Okay, Dad."

As I stand to leave, I watch for any sign that my mother wants to speak to me, but I see nothing. She never turns her head and says not a word. I can't leave things like this, though. I don't know if it will help anything, but I have to try to make her understand how terrible I feel about what I've done.

"Mom, I'm really sorry. I never wanted to lie to you. I didn't do it for any reason other than I guess I wasn't thinking about the consequences and what would happen when the truth came out. I'm so sorry I hurt you, Mom."

Tears begin to well in her eyes, but she never moves a muscle. She merely stares straight ahead, but as I walk past her, I swear I see her wince, like all of this is too much. Fuck, I've never felt so bad in my life.

My father sits in his favorite chair in the house, the black leather recliner that used to be in the living room until my mother bought all new furniture and exiled everything old to charity or my father's office. I practically collapse in the light blue upholstered chair he originally bought for this room, the one he hated from the first time he sat in it and decided never to use again.

"So, I found you an attorney I think will be able to

do the job. Andrew Correlli. I've known him since the Club X days, and he's exactly what you need."

Typical Cassian March. If there's a problem, you find someone who can solve it. No muss, no fuss. Just solve the damn problem so we can move the hell on.

"Thanks, Dad. I appreciate everything you're doing. The lawyer. Letting me stay here. I know none of this can be easy for you guys."

I want to say more, but somehow, the words get caught in my throat. I look away, unable to face him because unlike my mother, I know my father has things he wants to say to me.

"Cash, we'll handle this like we've handled everything else in this family before this. Kane is happy to run the restaurant so I can take some time off, and Stefan was the one who suggested Andrew to me. He got your uncle out of a couple jams a few years ago."

Hanging my head, I close my eyes as the reality that every member of the March and Jackson family knows what I've done. Jesus. No wonder my mother can't even look at me now.

"Thanks."

That's another typical Cassian March behavior. Get the entire family in on everything. Good, bad, it doesn't matter. If it's happening to one of us, it's happening for all of us. Never before have I wished for a much smaller family.

"Don't worry, son. I know things look bleak now, but they'll get better. You didn't kill anyone. You didn't rob a bank. It'll be okay."

I look up, surprised at my father's very untypical chipper outlook on things. "And Mom? Do you think she's ever going to speak to me again? I'd be happy if I could just get her to look at me, to be honest."

A look of sadness crosses my father's face as he nods. "Your mother needs some time. Just so you know, it isn't the getting arrested part that upsets her. After hearing the stories my mother told her when they met, I think your mother assumed the police would be a focal point of our lives, especially considering your uncles and I were still running Club X. No, it's not the illegal part of this that's bothering her. It's that you lied about going to law school and let her believe you were going to graduate in a few months."

"I know she really wanted me to be a lawyer, but I hope she can understand I hated the idea of living my life that way. It just wasn't for me."

My father finally smiles and shakes his head. "It's not that your mother wanted you to be a lawyer. Yes, she was proud of you because you were in law school, but she'd be happy with whatever you chose to do with your life. What's hurting her is you lied for all this time. She feels tricked, like she's been played for a fool. That's what's getting her."

"I never wanted to do that, Dad. The right time never came around, and then after a while, it seemed like it was too late to tell the truth. I knew I'd have to. Alex told me I had to tell her I wasn't graduating next spring, but I thought I had more time, I guess."

Surprise fills my father's eyes at the mention of my brother. "He knew this whole time?"

Quickly, I move to clear up his mistake. The last thing I want to do is drag my brother into my mess. "No, no. I just told him the last time I was down for the party at Grandma's. He couldn't believe it either."

"Your brother's getting better at keeping secrets, it seems," my father says with a chuckle. "When he was a little boy, he used to tell on you every time. Did you know that?"

Now it's my turn to be surprised. My little brother ratted me out when we were kids. I had no idea.

"No. I think I just figured you guys always found out because I wasn't good at hiding things. Wait until the next time I see him."

"Be good to your brother. He kept your secret this time, so obviously, he's grown out of the tattling stage."

"Well, it only took twenty-three years."

As if on cue, my brother pokes his head into the room and flashes us one of his trademark Alex March smiles. "Talking about me or someone else who just happens to be twenty-three years old?"

"What are you doing here?" I ask.

He steps into my father's office and closes the door behind him. "Well, the March family cavalry is here to rescue you. Hell of a crowd outside, though, and getting through it was a challenge. Thankfully, Cade, Liam, and I came in one car, so we didn't have to do our own version of a parade through those crazy people. We thought you might need some company."

I look over at my father to see him shrugging. "Don't look at me. I have to go try to talk your mother into forgiving you, so you four go outside to the pool and stay out of sight. Try not to seem like you're having the time of your life either, okay? She's not going to want to let you back in if she thinks you aren't really sorry."

"Thanks, Dad. You're the best. I don't know how I'm ever going to be able to repay you for all you're doing."

"It's what you do for family, Cash. Nothing more. Now go relax with your brother and your cousins. We have a big day ahead of us tomorrow when we go to meet with Andrew, so you need to be at your best."

Alex waves me toward him and opens the door to show Cade and Liam standing in the hallway. "See? We've come to save the day!"

As much as he may want to think hanging out with them can do that, I'm not sure that's going to be enough this time.

CHAPTER SIX

ash

THE THREE MEN SITTING IN FRONT OF ME STARE LIKE they aren't sure what they can say or where they should start. Do they want to ask me questions about the trouble I've gotten myself into or bust my balls about it? I can't tell by the way they're not saying anything for the past few minutes.

"Well, let it out," I say, leaning back on the deck chair and closing my eyes to let the sun warm my face. "Whatever you're going to say, just say it already."

But they don't say a word. In the silence, I hear what sounds like muffled laughter, so I open my eyes to see Cade with his hand covering his mouth and clearly enjoying himself.

"Since no one else seems to want to say it, I will. In my next life, I want to come back as you, Cash. You've got balls the size of Texas thinking you could get away with this."

"Think your girlfriend would like to hear you talking about wanting to be me?" I ask, busting his ass right back.

Cade smiles and shakes his head. "That's why I said in my next life. I don't know if Hailey and I will be together as our reincarnated selves, so if not, I definitely want to come back as Cash March, you sly bastard."

Leave it to Cade to start the ball rolling with that. Like being me right now is anything anyone would want.

"I'm just blown away about the whole not being in law school part," Liam says. "How long have you been lying about that?"

I put up two fingers and shrug. "Two years. Maybe a little more or less. It's been a long time, though."

"No wonder you looked like you were going to crawl out of your skin at the party the last time we were all out at Grandma's. All your mother could talk about was your graduation party. I just figured you weren't sure you were going to pass a class or something," Liam says before taking a drink of a beer. "Now it all makes sense."

The four of us fall silent for a few minutes before Alex finally grabs a beer and downs half of it like he's the one who's looking at prison time. "What I want to know is how much money there is in escorting women around town. And are they all old ladies like you always see in movies with escorts, or were they hot?"

Cade, Liam, and I all turn to look at my brother, and Cade says, "Ladies and gentlemen, Alex March cuts to the core of the whole deal and finally we get to the good stuff. So what's it like? I'm thinking lots of old women, right?"

I can't keep the smile from my face as I shake my head and prepare to divulge the truth of what it's like to run an escort service. "Not exactly. At first, it was only girls from law school. That's how it all got started. My friend Damon and I helped a girl we knew one time, and she told her friends who needed dates for some family things, and it took off from there. He and I didn't do much of the escorting, though. We were the managers of the guys who did. We'd hire them based on how they looked and if they had any special attributes our clients liked, such as being athletic looking or a certain ethnicity, and then I'd assign them to the women who called in looking for escorts. There were some older ones, but most were young like us, women who weren't interested in anything long-term when it came to guys but wanted a date for social events like weddings."

Alex narrows his eyes and leans forward toward me, like he's studying me. "So you didn't do any escorting at all?"

Cade and Liam lean in toward me too, like this is the stuff they came to hear. Shaking my head, I smile.

"I didn't say none at all. I did a couple dates, and at the end there, I did a wedding when I couldn't find anyone else to take the job over the holiday weekend. Nice woman too. Really sweet."

They all stare at me like they're waiting for me to say something else. I assume they want dirt, but that's not what the escort business was. At least not for me.

"Yeah, yeah. Get to the good stuff," Cade says impatiently. "Were you getting more ass than a toilet seat or what? I'm not buying that you were just some scheduling guy, Cash. We know you. There's no way you weren't dipping into the company's profits, so to speak."

I expect Liam and Alex to give Cade the signal that this isn't what they're here for, but they simply sit waiting for me to answer. I guess everyone does want the dirt, after all.

"That was never the main point of what Damon and I were doing. Believe it or not, we were in it to make money. It was a business, so we only hired people we thought would be what customers wanted and we made sure everyone knew they were supposed to act like professionals when they were out on assignments."

My answer seems to disappoint Cade, who slumps back in his chair like he expected to hear juicier stories. Liam and Alex look at each other and shrug, probably thinking my incredibly clinical description of what I've been up to is really very typical of me.

"Leave it to you to have a stable of guys you hire out to women and not enjoy the fruits of your labor," Cade says with a huff of disgust.

"So what's going to happen with the cops and the charges?" Liam asks before taking another drink of beer. "Knowing this state, they're probably clutching their fucking pearls at the idea of what you've been up to."

For the first time since the cops showed up in the parking lot of my building, I think about what's really going to happen and don't know how to answer my cousin. I honestly have no clue.

"I don't know. I guess if this lawyer I'm going to see tomorrow can't work some kind of magic, I'm looking at going to jail."

Even as I say that, I can't believe those words are coming out of my mouth. Going to jail. I can't believe that. How the fuck am I going to go to jail?

No wonder my mother looks like someone died. Instead of attending my graduation party in a few months, she's going to be sitting in a courtroom watching my trial and probably my conviction on all those charges.

"Cheer up, Cash," my brother says in that way he has of making everything sound like it's going to be okay. "They haven't found you guilty yet."

"Thanks, man. And thanks to you guys for coming over as the cavalry. Sorry I don't have any real spicy stories to tell."

Cade and Liam stand from their chairs to leave. "We should have known better than to believe all that bullshit the news is saying. This is Cash March we're talking about," Cade says with a laugh.

"Call us if you need anything, okay?" Liam says as he walks past me, patting me on the shoulder.

"Maybe you should tell Wilder to come over and give me some tips for when I get to jail," I joke.

"We'll stop over tomorrow or the next day, depending on how hard it is to get through the parking lot out on your street," Cade calls back as he walks into the house.

Left alone with Alex, I can't help but worry that no matter how much the four of us have a good time with everything that's happened, I'm still looking at the very real possibility that I might be locked up over what I've done. It may not have been as sexy as the news is making it out to be, but it's illegal and enough that I could be looking at some real time.

My brother pushes against my forearm, rousing me from some pretty terrible fucking thoughts about my future. When I look over at him, he smiles and holds up a cold beer.

"You look like you could use a new one. Don't worry, Cash. Everything's going to be okay."

As I take the bottle of beer from him, I force a smile. "You sure about that?"

He gives me a confident nod. "It always is for you. You're golden, Cash. You always have been. It'll work out. I know it will."

I'm golden. He's right. I always have been. Everything I've ever touched worked out just the way I wanted it to. School, work, girls. They all turned out exactly how I planned.

Then I got to law school and all that changed. I hated learning about all that shit attorneys need to know. I couldn't get out of those classes fast enough. And since I graduated from college, the whole women thing hasn't been terrific either. Too much time spent with Emily made me jaded and blasé about the idea of ever settling down with anyone.

So much for being fucking golden.

Lifting my bottle, I tap the neck off the top of Alex's bottle. "From your lips to God's ears. I've never wanted you to be right more than this time."

I take a gulp of beer and let it roll down my throat before saying to him, "The worst part of this is what it's done to Mom. That's what I'm most sorry about."

"She'll come around. Just wait a little while. Things will get better. If you like, you can stay at my place. I have a couch and it might be good to give her some space."

"That sounds great, but it might mean that all those news vultures outside follow us there. Are you ready for that?"

Alex waves away any thought that would bother him. "I don't care. You forget I have security at my place. Plus, they probably haven't even figured out we're related. I don't look like you. They probably think Liam is your brother since you guys look more alike than you and I do."

I shake my head at how true that is. "They're probably following him back to his apartment right now. Talk about bad luck genetics style, huh?"

My brother nods. "It might be good if they left, you know, for Mom's sake?"

That I hadn't thought about. He's right. At least if I could lure them away so she didn't have to see a crowd of people camped out at the end of the driveway, she might be able to forget about everything that's happened.

For a little while, at least.

"Maybe I will take you up on that offer."

Alex flashes me a big smile. "Great! I'm going to go talk to Dad, but I'll come back out to say goodbye before I go. You want to come over tonight or wait until tomorrow?"

"I have the meeting with that lawyer Dad found tomorrow morning, so let's say after that."

He stands to head inside and tosses me his keys. "Just in case you said yes, I came prepared. Come over whenever you want. I have to be at work by noon, so I'll be up early."

I look up at my younger brother and have to admit I got lucky. He could be like Wilder. That would suck.

"Thanks, Alex. And thanks for cheering me up."

"No thanks needed, Cash. You're my brother. You'd have my back if I was the one in your place."

As he walks away, I nod. That's the truth. We may be like night and day, but I'd lay it all on the line for him and all of my family. That's why I have to find a way to make things right.

I slide my phone out of my pocket and wish I'd see Savannah's name in my missed calls, but she's not there. Not surprising since she only has the burner phone number. I scroll through my notes and find her number, unsure I should call her now.

Fuck, who am I kidding? I'm not sure I should ever call her again since she probably hates me for lying to her, and that's saying nothing of how she likely feels about being roped into this huge scandal because of me. Calling her would be a mistake.

Yet, I can't stop myself. Even if I could simply hear her voice answering my call and then hang up, at least that would be something.

My fingers shake as I press the numbers into my phone and then bring it to my ear. She may not even answer if she's angry enough to never want to speak to me again. My chest tightens as her phone rings for the third time. She doesn't want to talk to me.

Then suddenly, I hear her say my name. "Cash? Are you there?" she asks sweetly, and my heart begins to beat again.

"Hi, Savannah. It's me."

"I've been so worried. Where are you?"

I look around my parents' backyard and smile. "I'm back in Tampa. I'm staying with my parents. It seemed like a good idea to get away for a while, but now that I'm down here, it's not really better. The media is camped out in front of the house. I barely was able to drive up to the house without running anyone over."

This probably isn't what she wants to talk about, but I can't stop myself from filling in all the empty space with these useless details. I don't want to give her a chance to tell me she never wants to hear from me again.

"Am I supposed to call you Cash, or is it Cassian?" Savannah asks, and in an instant, everything I wanted to say disappears from my brain.

I hang my head, hating that she's doubting even

my name. What else must she be thinking wasn't real between us?

"It's Cash. I didn't lie about that. Only my last name. That's my mother's maiden name, so it's technically still in the family."

As if that means a goddamned thing.

"And the fact that you weren't just an escort but the owner of the business?"

Co-owner, but now doesn't seem like the right time to get mired down in semantics.

"Right, but everything else was the truth. I swear, Savannah. I didn't lie about anything else. Just those two things."

The phone falls silent, and I wonder if she left without even saying goodbye. I deserve it. I just hoped that maybe when she heard me apologize she wouldn't want to give up on us.

I wait for her to say something, afraid to check to see if she's still there and find she's gone. My heart slams into my chest, racing in anticipation of the next thing I'll hear.

Finally, she says quietly, "Really? You didn't lie about anything else?"

My spirits soar. She hasn't given up on us, on me, yet. I still have a chance to make her understand how much she means to me.

"I swear, Savannah, I didn't lie when we were together. The stories I told you about my family were real. How I acted when I was with you was real. I loved spending time with you. That day at the beach was the most fun I've had in a long time. I'm so sorry this all happened."

Again, she falls silent. I don't want to give her a chance to end the call, so I keep talking, hoping she'll listen and say something else. Something like she still cares about me too.

"I know you must have been so scared when the cops took me away like they did. I hate that you were left all alone there. I never wanted that to happen."

"It wasn't so bad. I called my sister Cheyenne, and she came to pick me up. I was just so worried about you. When I saw those handcuffs on your wrists, I felt like crying."

She does still care. Knowing that makes me feel like Alex might be right. Maybe everything will be okay.

"I know, and I'm sorry you had to see that. I keep saying I'm sorry, but I feel like I have to apologize for so much, Savannah. You should have never had to go through that, and what the media is doing to you now is all my fault. Are you okay?"

I hear a tiny sigh and know she's not, no matter what kind of brave front she puts on.

"My attorney doesn't think what they're saying on the news will actually happen. I can't imagine them rounding up all the women and arresting us like I heard they would. It's just a nuisance to have them all waiting outside for any chance to ask me all those questions. I want to scream every time I open the front door."

"I'm sorry."

God, I wish I had something else to say to her. All I seem to be able to do is tell her I'm sorry. I can't fix anything for her. I can't make it better. All I can do is say those two damn words over and over.

She deserves better than this. She deserves better than me. It's time I admit that and let her go. No matter how much it fucking hurts, it's the least I can do for her now.

"Well, I just wanted to check up on you to make sure you're getting through all this okay. I don't expect to be able to call you much from now on, so I wanted to say a proper goodbye. You and I had a nice time together, and you shouldn't have to deal with all of what's going on, but I think it's better this way."

Every word feels like someone's shoving a knife into my heart. I sound so goddamned flippant, like she was nothing but a good lay. I really can be a son of a bitch sometimes.

The hurt from what I'm saying comes through loud and clear when she asks, "So you called to say goodbye? Is that what this is?"

"Well, you know how it is."

That sentence means nothing, and I don't even know why I'm saying things like that. I just don't know how to let her go, so now I'm simply filling the space with nonsense.

She so doesn't deserve that either.

"I thought you said you didn't lie about anything else, Cash. You made me think you cared about me, and now all you can say is you're sorry and goodbye? Why are you doing this?"

I don't have any good answers for her, so I say, "I have to go. Good luck, Savannah. If they ask me about you, I promise I'll make sure they think there was nothing between us. You'll be safe from that, at least. Goodbye."

Pulling the phone from my ear, I end the call as I hear her begin to say something. It doesn't matter. After all that's happened, this is for the best.

She deserves better than what I can offer her.

CHAPTER SEVEN

ash

ANDREW CORELLI'S OFFICE LOOKS LIKE WHAT I imagine my mother thought my office would look like someday. Lots of polished wood and a desk that I'm guessing is about the size of a studio apartment. Bookshelves with volume after thick volume sit behind him, like an advertisement for how intelligent and educated he is. Most appear to be related to his profession, but as I glance down toward the lower shelves, I notice some that look distinctly not like what an attorney would spend his workday reading.

He stops talking to my father and smiles as I focus on those titles. "My son is five. His favorite books are anything Dr. Seuss. Just in case you were having second thoughts about my ability to handle your case. Trust me, if I never read another Dr. Seuss book again in my life, I'd be the happiest man in the world. However, since my wife is pregnant with twins, I suspect chances are at least one of them is going to like these books too. My future reading choices look rather bleak."

"Well, I know all about bleak futures, so I can sympathize," I say, pushing myself to smile since it seems like my lawyer is trying to lighten the mood.

My misery makes him smile, much like it always has with my brother. Correlli actually sort of reminds me of Alex with his dark brown eyes and way of talking that makes everything seem so casual and easy. Dressed in a white dress shirt, a blue tie with grey diamond shapes, and black suit pants, he looks like Alex did the last time someone forced him to get dressed up.

Waving away my worries about what my future may hold and how it looks like it may involve a lengthy prison sentence, he lets out a belly laugh that surprises me since he's a rail thin man. "All is not lost, so don't go jumping off any bridges any time soon. I haven't given up on this entire issue being handled quite easily, so you don't give up either."

I want to believe him, but at the moment, that hint of happiness seems next to impossible. The issue can be handled quite easily? Is that really going to happen?

"Really?" I ask in amazement, interested in hearing more about how my life isn't completely ruined.

Correlli leans back against his expensive office chair with the superior lumbar support and puts his hands behind his head as a sign of confidence. "Really," he says with a broad smile. "They've got little in the way of evidence that any money ever came into your hands, which by the way, was a stroke of brilliance. You and your friend were incredibly smart to do things that way. Without the money issue clouding everything up, the federal tax evasion case falls apart and the issue of prostitution disappears too. No money means nobody sold anything, sex or otherwise."

"That was Damon's idea, to be honest," I admit, happy to know the whole cryptocurrency and funneling the proceeds from the business through two offshore accounts before it ends up in a third for each of us turned out to be more than a lot of work.

"Well, Damon is a bright man. I've spoken to his attorney, and he's feeling the same way. No money trail means no crimes. However, let me be careful not to let you think it's impossible to find said money. The local and state police might struggle, but the Feds have a way of ferreting out the truth of the matter, so don't go celebrating just yet."

My father turns to look at me, and for the first time since I saw him standing outside my car yesterday, he looks like himself. I even see a hint of hopefulness in his eyes. I just pray it isn't all taken away from him if the Feds find that proof.

"I told you Andrew would know what to do."

"Your father and I go way back. He and your uncles were a handful when they were your age. You know, just in case anyone wants to say they can't believe you did what you did. The apple doesn't fall far from the tree," Correlli jokes.

"It must run in the genes," my father says with a chuckle. "Cash here just sounds like he brought it into the twenty-first century."

Forcing a smile, I try to laugh, but I don't have the ability to joke around about how badly I've fucked up my life. Not yet, anyway. Maybe if and when the charges are dropped and all the people caught up in this mess have their charges dropped, then I can have a good laugh about it all.

Correlli's mood changes quickly, and he sits forward in his chair and levels his gaze on me, as if the time for getting serious has finally arrived. "Okay, this is what you're going to do while I handle my end of this. You're not to contact anyone from the business. Not Damon. No one you worked with. Not a soul."

Instantly, any shred of light I was clinging to seems to go dark. "Why? Damon would be okay. He's in the same boat as me."

That doesn't matter, as far as I can tell by the way the lawyer shakes his head. "Nope. Any one of those people can be a witness against you. Trust me. Damon's attorney is telling him the same thing, so it's not like you guys are abandoning one another. We need to compartmentalize everything and keep you away from everyone."

Someone knocking on his office door interrupts our discussion, and an elderly man with gray hair and bushy eyebrows pokes his head in through the crack in the door. "Andrew, do you have a minute? I've got something I need to discuss with you."

Correlli nods and stands from his chair. "Relax for a few moments, and I'll be right back, gentlemen."

Once my father and I are alone, he gives my arm a nudge and asks, "Why are you concerned about talking to anyone associated with the business? Do you think Damon is going to roll on you?"

I don't have to think for more than a second about that question to answer with more confidence than I have about most things in my life. Shaking my head, I say, "No. That's not it. Damon's good. He's not going to rat me out for anything."

Confusion fills my father's eyes. "Then what's up?"

"Well, I feel bad for those guys. Not Damon but the other guys who worked for us. They don't deserve what's happening to them. Then there are the women the news says the cops are going to go after. That's not right."

"But I thought you told me you didn't do any of the actual escorting. How would you know any of them other than by their names?"

With a sigh, I let out a tiny fraction of the worry I have about one of those women. "I didn't until the very end. Her name is Savannah. She's a nice person, and I hate that she's been dragged into this."

My father studies me for a long moment before a tiny smile breaks up his usual serious expression. "Sounds like more than an escorting thing to me."

"She is. Was," I admit, hating that I have to change the tense of that verb from present to past.

Thankfully, the lawyer returns before my father can really begin interrogating me about Savannah. "Sorry about that. Now where were we? Oh, yes. No contacting anyone from the business. No Damon. No guys."

And then, out of the blue, my father says, "What about any friends who he might have met through the business?"

What the fuck is he doing?

I turn my head to look at him and my mouth drops open in shock. Why would he ask that? What's he thinking?

"By the way Cash is gaping at you, I'm assuming you're not asking because he wasn't sure he should, Cassian."

My father smiles at me like he's proud of himself. "I was just curious. I thought it was a question that should be asked."

"It didn't," I curtly say, pissed he's opened up this can of worms right here in the damn lawyer's office.

The three of us fall silent for a few moments, but Correlli finally clears his throat and says, "Okay, here's something else you're going to do. Or not going to do. No calling anyone at all. Speak only to family."

I nod, silently thinking to myself that I wasn't planning on calling Savannah again anyway.

That doesn't seem to be good enough for him, though, and his expression twists into a grimace. "On second thought, you're going to leave your phone with me."

I stare across the desk at him in shock. I feel like

I'm at the principal's office being punished for being bad in class.

"What? Why?"

"Just hand it over. It's for the best. Trust me."

But that doesn't sound good enough for me. "The cops already took my phone when they brought me in. Whatever's on it, they know about and I'm happy to tell you about."

Correlli sticks his hand out toward me. "I know what the police did. I'm trying to make sure you don't endanger this case and your freedom, Cash. Turn it off and give it to me."

I feel my father's stare practically burning a hole in the left side of my face, and I turn to look at him. The lawyer wouldn't be asking for my goddamned phone if he hadn't brought up the subject of me calling people back in Gainesville.

"Come on, Cash. If Andrew thinks this is necessary, then you have to do it."

As I fish my phone out of my pants pocket, I mumble, "It wouldn't be necessary if you didn't feel the need to ask your questions."

After I turn it off, I hand it to the lawyer and watch him put it in his desk drawer. The smile on his face says he's happy, and out of the corner of my eye, I see my father looks pleased too.

How nice for both of them.

"Okay, let me get to working on things, and Cash, you stay low. Talk only to your family, and let me see what I can do."

My father stands to give Correlli a handshake and

they joke about something in their past I know nothing about. I just want to get the hell out of this place and somewhere I can be alone. I don't want to talk to anyone, including my family, at this moment.

When the lawyer grabs my hand to shake it, I force myself to smile. "Don't worry, Cash. Just take it easy until I contact you. No need to stress out yet. We're still in the first quarter of this game."

His odd sports reference makes him and my father laugh, but I find nothing about it funny. I'm officially a man who can't go home, can't speak to anyone other than his family members, and has been thrown back to the time before cell phones.

Ironic for a guy who used to have multiple phones and spent his days running an entire business on them.

AFTER A DRIVE BACK TO THE HOUSE FULL OF silence on my part and chatter about March family gossip I don't care about meant to fill the dead space on my father's part, we walk into the house to find my mother sitting exactly where we left her hours ago on the couch staring at the TV. I look at her and wonder if she's moved at all since I attempted to talk to her yesterday.

I have to try again, though. Maybe if she hears how the meeting went with the lawyer, she'll cheer up and finally say something to me.

My father disappears to his office, so I quietly take a seat across from her on the same chair I sat in yesterday when I tried this the first time. Perhaps the second time will be the charm.

"Hey, Mom. We met with the lawyer Dad knows. Interesting guy. Has what might be considered an irrational hatred for Dr. Seuss."

Nothing. She doesn't blink, and I see not a single facial muscle move even the tiniest bit. She looks like a stone statue.

"So he doesn't think it will turn out so bad after all. He even mentioned the idea that all the charges might be dropped. That's good news, isn't it?" I say, all chipper and hoping against hope she'll have some reaction.

Anything would do at this point.

But again, she doesn't respond at all.

I turn to look at what's on the TV and watch it for a few seconds. It's some cooking show with a woman whose eyes appear to bug out of her head every time she adds an ingredient to her recipe and whose voice sounds like she's gargling rocks at the end of each sentence. Who the hell would give this woman a cooking show, and why the hell would anyone watch this?

Then the awful truth dawns on me. My mother would prefer to watch this show with this woman and her grating voice than even exchange a word of conversation with her older son.

Desperation fills me as I stare at the woman who cleaned my scraped knees and dried my tears when I got hurt as a boy. She can't hate me that much that she never wants to talk to me again.

Can she?

I've never seen her like this. On the outside, she looks just like she always has. Her red hair and pale skin haven't changed since I was a little boy and other kids' moms would point out Olivia March wherever we were and mention how lovely she was. She's still as beautiful today, even now as her mouth turns down into a frown I'm afraid will be there permanently because of me.

I watch her dark brown eyes for any sign she cares that I'm right here, just feet away from her, but they seem dimmer than usual. There's a flatness to them I've never seen before. It doesn't make her any less beautiful, but it creates a sense of utter sadness in her expression that I don't think I can bear for much longer, especially because I'm the reason it's there at all.

Finally, I have to look away, unable to see that in her anymore. "I'm so sorry, Mom. I wish I could make you see that I feel terrible about what I've done to you and Dad. I never meant to hurt you. That's the last thing in the world I would ever want to do. Please know that. I just wish you'd talk to me. Say something. Tell me how stupid I am or tell me how angry you are with me. I deserve it all. Just say something, Mom. I hate to see you like this, and I know I'm the one who made you feel this way, but say something. Please."

For a few moments, I stare at the tan carpeting my mother had installed once Alex and I moved out and she knew we wouldn't make any more messes that would ruin the house. Now, though, I've brought a mess to this place that can't be fixed by buying new furniture or changing out the carpeting.

I lift my head and see her staring at me. The hurt in her eyes kills me, and I immediately have to look away again. I wait for her to say something, but all I get is silence.

When I turn back to face her, she's still just staring at me like she's been staring at the woman with the awful voice cook some salmon recipe. She doesn't move, but I think at any moment she might break into tears.

"Mom, please, I'm sorry. Say something. You've always been the one who talks. Dad doesn't say a word when he's angry, but this time he's the one doing the talking. Please say something."

She says nothing. I glance up over her head to see my father standing behind the sofa shaking his head.

"I'm going to let you get back to your show, Mom. If you want to talk to me, just yell my name, okay?"

As I get up to leave, she turns back to the TV. She won't be yelling for me anytime soon.

My father wraps his arm around my shoulder and ushers me down the hall toward his office. "You have to give your mother a little time, Cash. This is how she is when she's hurt. She shuts down. It's her way of defending herself against getting hurt even more."

"I've never seen her like this. She's never not spoken to me for this long. I'd expect that from you, to be honest, but not her. Not Mom," I say as we sit down across from one another in his office.

He nods his understanding. "I've only seen it a couple times in all the years I've known her. The first time was when I messed up when we were dating. I was used to women screaming and yelling, but that's not your mother's style. She shut down and closed herself off, and let me tell you, I nearly lost my mind. I called and called, but it didn't work. I went over to her apartment, and it didn't work. But I didn't give up."

His point is coming through loud and clear. I can't give up either. I fucked up, and of all the people I need to make amends to, my mother is at the top of the list.

"Okay, Dad. I get what you're saying. I was going to go to stay with Alex since he offered and I thought it would be better since I don't want to upset Mom, but I'm going to stay right here and keep trying to make her see I know I screwed up."

My father purses his lips and then blows the air out of his lungs. "Actually, Cash, I think this time calls for the opposite approach. Give your mother some space. If Alex is offering, go stay with him. I have a feeling that will be better for both of you."

Disappointment washes over me at the reality that the one thing that's worked in the past to make my mother feel better again won't work this time. I really fucked up if trying won't help.

"Okay, Dad. Alex said I could come over this morning after we got done with Correlli, so I think I'll get my bag and head out now. Since I don't have my cell, if you need me, I guess call Alex's."

I don't say the words, but I hope he understands that if my mother even utters a syllable about wanting to talk to me, I want him to find a way to get in touch with me because I'll rush back here in a heartbeat just to talk to her.

"I will, Cash. Don't worry. She just needs some time. Give her some time and I bet you two will be back to talking again before you know it."

Forcing a smile, I try to make him think I believe that. "Yeah, I bet you're right. At least when I go, I'll take that traveling circus living outside at the curb with me. At least there's that, right?"

With a laugh, he reminds me of something that had slipped my mind when Alex offered to let me stay with him. "Thank God your brother chose to live in a place with a gate and security to get in. I bet he never thought he'd need that, but it's good luck he has it now."

I smile, knowing the real reason Alex chose to live in a place with that much security. My brother has a habit of hooking up with women who get a little obsessed with him. It's like he has a radar and seeks these women out. On the surface, they look normal, if not a little odd because they also tend to have some strange interests, but it doesn't take long to realize they're crazy.

Security was the biggest selling point of his building, especially considering his apartment isn't much to look at. But I'll let my father think it's just a happy coincidence.

The less our parents know about what we're really like in our personal lives, the better. This mess I'm in just proves that.

CHAPTER EIGHT

*S*avannah

BEING TRAPPED IN YOUR HOUSE IS ALL IT'S CRACKED up to be. Awful and maddening are the two best ways to describe it. I wander around from room to room wishing I could go somewhere, even though on most days I'd normally choose to stay home.

I peer out from behind the curtains at the swarm of reporters waiting out on the street and feel my anger rise inside me. Yesterday I was calling them a crowd. Today the group has grown to a swarm. Not that a few more matters. Unless they all disappear, even a handful would keep me trapped in my house.

What I wouldn't give to be at the beach today. I never loved the beach, but that day I spent with Cash lying on that towel barely big enough for the two of us, our toes buried in the sand and the scent of sunscreen filling my nose makes me think that's exactly the place I'd like to be right now.

Only if I could be with him, though.

"Savannah, where are you? That Dudley guy is here to see you," Cheyenne calls out from the kitchen.

Dutmeyer. Robert Dutmeyer. She insists on calling him by the wrong name, even though she knows what the right one is. I swear she's just trying to press on my last nerve.

I stop myself before I open my bedroom door and yell out his correct name. Taking a deep breath, I remind myself that she's stuck here too because of this mess, and she can't be having a good time being trapped in the house for days on end.

By the time I make it to the kitchen, my urge to snap at her and repeat my lawyer's name a hundred times has subsided, thankfully. "Cheyenne, I'll be meeting with Mr. Dutmeyer on the back porch, if you want to join us. He might have something to say that could help you too since you insist on not hiring an attorney."

My sister shakes her head and frowns. "Just give me the high points when he leaves. By the way, he's up the driveway already, so he should be ringing the doorbell any moment now."

I quickly rush over to the refrigerator and grab the pitcher of lemonade I made right after he called to let me know he'd be stopping by this afternoon. When I spin around to set it on the island to find the tray and glasses, Cheyenne's standing there with them in her hands waiting for me.

"See? I'm just irritating some of the time. Other times, I can be extremely helpful."

Rolling my eyes, I smile. "Please make sure you don't call him by the wrong name to his face, okay? Imagine if someone called you Charlie or Charlene when they knew your real name."

She nods and gives me a little laugh. "Point taken. That would bug me to no end. I promise no more Dudley. It's just that name is so funny. Dudley. You hear it?"

I set the pitcher next to the glasses and head toward the porch at the back of the house with them on the tray. "You need to get out more. I think you're starting to go stir crazy."

"Tell me about it! Three days being cooped up in this house makes me feel like I'm going squirrely. How do you hang out here all the time?" she yells after me.

I don't answer her, but the truth is, I stay in because it's safe. No people do deal with. No issues. Just safety and relaxation. What's wrong with that?

The doorbell rings, so I call out, "Cheyenne, please let Mr. Dutmeyer is and bring him back here."

I hear her laugh and answer, "As you wish, madam. Maybe when all of this is over, you can hire a butler. How great would it be if his name was Dudley? I'd love that!"

If my lawyer wasn't on his way into the house, that comment right there would be enough for me to snap. Enough with the goddamned Dudley!

A minute later, Cheyenne appears in the doorway

with Robert. "Savannah, Mr. Dutmeyer for you. I'll be in my room if you need me."

My attorney looks as crisp and formal as he always does when I go to see him in his office. A longtime friend of my husband, he's an older man who dyes his hair dark brown but doesn't do anything with his ridiculously long and very gray eyebrows. The effect for the first few seconds every time I'm face to face with him is nothing less than jarring. Thankfully, he always wears the most impeccable Italian suits and striking silk ties, so I can shift my focus to them and not stare at the bizarre hair choices he insists on making.

"Good afternoon, Robert. Please, sit. I have fresh lemonade. Like usual, I love that tie. Are those turtles in that design? I love how the deep green and teal blue work together."

He smiles, flashing me a bright white smile of straight white dentures, and sits down across from me as he lifts his tie like he needs to look at it to be reminded exactly what the design is. "Yes, they are. My secretary bought it for me for my birthday. She's always so thoughtful."

I nod, remembering that this is the secretary who's twenty years younger than he is and the woman he takes on vacations anytime he goes away. Why he tells everyone they're simply employer and employee I don't understand.

Or maybe it's the age gap. But I thought men loved dating much younger women. No matter. She's his girlfriend, so he should just call her that.

After some small talk about Linda, his secretary, and how things have been since he and I have last spoken, he takes a deep breath in and sits back to let it out. I watch as he seems to struggle with what he wants to say. I guess I don't blame him. It's not every day a man like him has to broach the subject of an illegal escort service.

"So, I spoke to the police, and I don't believe they intend on doing anything to you or your sister."

This day is getting better already. "That's wonderful! Thank you, Robert. Whatever you did, thank you."

"I get the feeling that was more bluster than anything else, so I'm not sure I can take the credit for this turn of events. In fact, they seemed downright uncomfortable discussing the idea of coming to arrest you in particular, but that's probably because I spent the entire conversation with the detective and his captain reminding them of who you are and who your husband was. I sense they feel dragging you in like they did those young men would give the department a black eye."

Lifting my glass of lemonade, I toast his excellent ability to persuade. "To Robert, who clearly did do something when he made sure the Gainesville police department understood how awkward it would be to arrest the widow of Carson Gardener, one of the most popular men in town and a very generous contributor to every police effort."

Robert lifts his glass and smiles as he taps it off

mine. "I never even got to bring up how much Carson gave to the yearly policeman's ball."

"Then the police are very smart and you didn't need to. Thank you all the same, Robert. This whole thing is ridiculous to start with."

He takes a sip of his lemonade and sets his glass down on the table between us, suddenly far more serious than when we were discussing charges for Cheyenne and me. Shaking his head, he frowns.

"Ridiculous or not, they have a case against the two owners of the escort business. I suspect they're grilling all those young men they walked in front of the TV cameras yesterday hoping to find out some details. From what I hear, though, those March and Childress fellows played things very close to the vest. No one ever actually met either of them or knew their last names, so the first time they ever had a face to put with the first names was the other day when the cops swooped in and arrested them."

So much for this day turning out great.

I hate hearing that Cash might suffer because of this, no matter how illegal what they did was. All I know is they offered a service that people like my sister and I needed. It was never about prostitution or mere sex. What that escort service did was give us the chance to do things without having to answer a million questions about why we aren't married yet. For a single woman, that's worth its weight in gold.

"Robert, how bad are we talking?" I ask as my stomach twists into a tight knot.

"Bad. Let's just say I'm much happier being your attorney than theirs," he answers somberly.

"I want to help. Can I do anything? Tell me and I'll do it."

My lawyer shakes his head and recoils like this is the worst idea he's ever heard. "No. I want you to stay away from him. It will be better for everyone. No contact at all, Savannah. Do you hear me?"

The way he says that reminds me of how my father used to reprimand us kids when we did something wrong. He always ended his scolding with the words do you hear me. I always wanted to say that I wasn't deaf, and right now, I have to bite my tongue from saying the same thing as a grown woman.

I hear him. I just don't like the words he's saying.

"Fine."

Robert stands to leave and nods his head, clearly happy I've agreed to what he demands. I don't and haven't, but this isn't an argument I want to have with him right now.

"I'll let you know when I hear anything, but for now, I think you and Cheyenne are in the clear. Don't talk to the press outside your door, though, okay, Savannah? I know you want to. I know you want to tell them what's on your mind, but don't. It won't turn out well. And above all, no contacting anyone from that escort business. That's their mess to deal with now, not yours."

"Okay. Thank you, Robert. I appreciate your help with this."

"I'll see myself out. Cheer up, Savannah. Things can only get better."

That gets him a tepid smile. I guess he's right. I mean, could things get worse for Cash and me? First, there is no Cash and me as of the last time we talked. All he could say was I deserved better. Better than him. Better than this. Just better.

The problem is I don't want anyone else. I don't care if the world thinks some other more proper man would be better for me.

"So what did your fine lawyer have to say? Are we headed for the big house? They warn men not to drop the soap. What's the warning for women?"

I look up as the last thoughts of Cash drift away and see Cheyenne smiling down at me from the doorway. Dressed in her black bikini, she looks as relaxed as she always has, even joking about us going to prison.

"You ask the most bizarre questions. I love that bathing suit on you. Running has definitely paid dividends, I'd say."

She poses for a moment and her grin spreads practically ear to ear. "Thanks! I'll probably gain a ton of it back since I'm trapped at Chez Savannah until further notice. You really could use a treadmill here, you know."

"I'm not a runner, so all it would do is gather dust. By the way, Robert told me he thinks the police are going to drop this idea of charging any of us who used the service. I'd say that's good news."

Cheyenne strikes another pose to show off her

favorite bathing suit and points out toward the pool. "That calls for a swim. So I'll be free to move about the countryside soon? But if it's all good news, why do you look like someone just told you their aunt squandered all their money and they're broke?"

I wave off her question, not really wanting to talk about why I'm still sad after hearing Robert's news. The problem is Cheyenne isn't one to let anything go, so she pushes for an answer, like always.

Finally, after avoiding telling her the truth, I mumble, "I'm just missing Cash. I'm worried about him. I want to call him, but Robert says I shouldn't. Not that it matters since he doesn't want to see me anymore."

"Oh, honey, that's probably just what his lawyer told him to do like Dudley did. I say once you're sprung from our luxury jail here, you should find out where he is and go see him. Go after what you want, Savannah. It's the only way to ensure you find your happiness."

So typical Cheyenne. Nothing ever seems daunting to her.

"One problem. Well, more than one problem, but the big one is I don't know where he is and his phone is turned off."

"Hire a private detective. Put all that money to good use. Keep in mind that I might need to borrow a significant amount if my school fires me because of this whole escort thing," she says before tossing her towel over her shoulder.

"You don't exactly look worried about losing your

job. How do you do it?" I ask as she walks away toward the pool.

Cheyenne turns around and throws her towel on one of the chaise lounges. "What will happen will happen. I can't change that. If I could, I would, but I can't, so I'm going swimming. Want to join me?"

I shake my head at her way of just letting life happen without stressing her out. I wish I could be like her.

Spreading her arms out to the side, she lets herself fall backwards into the pool like she doesn't have a care in the world. God, I wish I was like her.

CHAPTER NINE

ash

THREE DAYS OF LAYING AROUND MY BROTHER'S
apartment avoiding the outside world has me feeling
like shit. Every day, he goes off to his job at the
restaurant while I stay here like some kind of man-
sized slug. My main exercise has been shuffling from
the couch to the kitchen and back again, and I think
I've watched every goddamned movie on Netflix.

Not exactly anything to brag about, especially
since I'm essentially hiding out here.

At least the media circus has all but gone away.
They followed me here when I left my parents' house,
but that security Alex thought would be useful only to
keep his crazy girlfriends at bay turned out to be the
trick I needed. Unable to get close to where I was, the
news crews slowly disappeared. When I looked out

this morning, there was one lonely reporter and a single news van and nothing else.

"Not that I don't appreciate your circumstances, but dude, you look like some kind of guy who's been living in the wild for half a year. Have you even brushed your teeth since you got here?"

I look up at Alex from my spot on the couch and narrow my eyes in disgust. "What's the fucking point of shaving if I'm just going to sit here and watch another eight movies today? As for my teeth, yes, I've brushed them. Who are you, my mother?"

My salty comeback leaves my mouth before I realize it, and Alex stares down at me like I'm some pathetic thing he wishes he could help. "Have you spoken to her since you've been here?"

I shake my head, hating that the truth of the matter is I haven't and I'm beginning to wonder if she's ever going to speak to me again in this lifetime. "No. Dad said to give her some space, so that's what I'm doing."

"Okay. I'm going to jump into the shower since I have to be at the restaurant earlier than my usual today."

Even that sounds more exciting than what I have planned for the next twelve hours. I think I might be growing roots into my brother's couch, so there's that, and I might choose to get so drunk that I forget what my life has become.

To think that I was a guy who had the world by the short hairs just a week ago.

All this time alone makes me want to do the one

thing I shouldn't do. I made sure to cut off things with Savannah in such a way that she shouldn't ever want to talk to me again, but that's all I can think of since I got here.

I can't give in to that. She's better off without me.

Leaning back against the couch, I close my eyes and wish I didn't miss her so damn much. My chest feels like someone's pressing down on it with a giant weight and I can't get a full breath of air in. Maybe it's this place. Being stuck inside a one bedroom apartment day after day could do that to a person. Not talking to anyone but Alex could do it too.

That's it. Maybe I just need to spend some time out on the balcony today. Get some fresh air. Get the fuck away from in front of the TV and every bad movie ever made.

When I open my eyes and look around at my brother's home, I know the truth. It won't matter how much fresh air I get or how many movies I don't watch. I'm still going to feel this way because I miss Savannah.

Across the room, his phone sits with his keys on the table where he routinely sets them before work. I listen for the sound of water from the shower, but I can't hear anything since the bathroom is on the other side of the apartment.

I jog down the hallway and press my ear to the door. Now I can hear the water running. Good! That means I have at least a few minutes while he finishes showering and then gets ready for work.

Quickly, I run back to get his phone and press in Savannah's number to send her a text.

I'm sorry for what I said the other night. I only wanted to protect you, but I know I hurt you. Don't call or text back since this isn't my phone, but I want to see you.

Sure the water has stopped running, I creep down the hallway again and listen. Fuck. Alex is done with his shower already. Damn! The one day I needed him to take a long shower he rushes through the thing.

I hurriedly type in his address and security code to give to the guy in the shack outside and tell her Alex will be gone for the night.

Please come. I miss you.

My hands shaking, I send the text and then quickly delete all proof both messages ever existed before setting his phone back exactly the way it was. I take my usual position on the couch and try to look as casual as possible. When he comes out to leave for work, I'm doing exactly what I've done every minute I've been here.

Watching TV from the end of the couch in his living room.

"Got any plans tonight?" Alex asks as he grabs his keys and stuffs his phone into his pants pocket.

I shrug like nothing means anything to me, even while I wonder if Savannah already got my text and is making plans to come down here at this very moment. "Just living the dream here on the third cushion of your luxurious couch. I might move to the second cushion, though, just to change things up a bit."

"Okay. Try not to have too much fun. I'll be back by a little after midnight, unless things get really wild. I don't think they will, but you never know. How about I grab some beer and we can get drunk since I have tomorrow off?"

I smile, thankful for his attempts at cheering me up. Alex is a good guy and a hell of a brother. He's also someone who hates to be around miserable people, so I imagine his efforts to get me drunk tonight are as much to rid himself of the frown he sees every time he lays eyes on me as they are to help me get out of this funk.

"Yeah, that might be good. I could go for a few beers."

"Good. I'll see you later then. Have a good night!"

As he walks out the door, I smile to myself. I hope I do have exactly that. I just need Savannah to show up.

I LET MY HEAD LOLL BACK ON THE ARM OF THE couch as the second Star Wars prequel ends with Anakin and Padme getting a brief moment of happiness. I could watch the third one, but my mood isn't anywhere it needs to be to see that romance and Anakin's friendship with Obi-Wan go up in smoke when he chooses the dark side.

Maybe I should find a comedy to watch.

A knock at the front door makes me sit up, and for a second, panic rushes through me. Did one of those media people make it through the security outside to get up here? Then I remember I texted Savannah to come down to see me. Did she actually do it?

I hurry to the door and look through the peephole to see her beautiful face. Dressed in white shorts, a navy blue t-shirt, and white sandals, she looks like sweetness personified. But she looks unsure, like she doesn't know if she should be here or maybe she made a mistake coming to see me. I have to stop her before she runs away.

Throwing open the door, I grab her arm and pull her inside. "You came! I wasn't sure you would, but I'm so happy to see you. Come in!"

When I close the door, she wraps her arms around my neck and hugs me tightly to her. "Cash, I missed you so much. I've been so worried about you. Then all those things you said the other night made me wish I could see you so we could talk, but I kept calling your phone and it went directly to voicemail. I thought you were avoiding me."

I revel in the feel of her body next to mine. God, I've missed her. She's soft and delicate, but just having her with me gives me the strength I need to go on. For the first time since those cops took me away, I honestly believe I can get through this.

She clings to me, refusing to let go, and I inhale a deep breath to take in the soft scent of her perfume. It instantly reminds me of the time we spent together at her house, something I pray to God I might have the chance to do again.

"I'm so sorry, Savannah. I should have never said

all those things the other day. I thought I was doing the right thing, but I've been miserable ever since."

Her body trembles, and then I feel her crying. "Cheyenne said I should find out where you are and go to you, but I didn't know how to do that. I wasn't sure which name to search, and she said I should hire a private investigator. Then I got your text and it felt like it was sent from heaven. I got in my car and drove as fast as I could to get here."

I pry her hands from my neck and lean back to look down at her beautiful face. It's wet with tears, so I gently run the pads of my thumbs across the tops of her cheeks to dry them. I feel like she's heaven sent, an angel come to make everything better.

Cradling her face, I kiss her softly on the lips, and she lets out a sigh. I know exactly how she feels. It's like everything will be okay now that we're together again.

"I think proper introductions are in order. I'm Cash March, not Cash Lucas, Lucas is my mother's maiden name. You already know this next part, but I wasn't just an escort. I was the co-owner of the business. That doesn't change anything that happened between us, though, Savannah. The only time I was working was when I was your date for your brother's wedding. Everything after that was just me wanting to be with you."

She smiles after a few seconds of taking all that information in and runs her hand along my jaw covered in a new beard. "Cassian March IV is what they keep calling you on the news. It sounds very formal and nothing like the man I know."

"My given name after my father, my grandfather, and my great-grandfather."

Her dark eyes search my face for a moment before she nods. "It's a very nice name. Very regal. I think I like Cash better, though. You'll always be Cash to me."

"I'm so sorry you got caught up in my mess. I never wanted you to get hurt. Not by me and not with the police. If I could go back in time and change things, I would make sure you never got involved with the escort service. You or your sister."

Hurt fills her expression, and she shakes her head. "Don't say that! If I didn't call that number, I would have never met you. Are you saying you wish we never met?"

Jesus, I keep screwing things up. I can't even say what I mean without it coming out wrong.

"No, not at all. I just wish you didn't have all those people outside your home sticking microphones in your face whenever you open the door. I hate the idea that the police are going to drag you into this. You shouldn't have to deal with any of it. That's all I meant."

Suddenly, a smile brightens her face. "My attorney says that the police aren't going to come after the women who used the escort service, so I think we're going to be safe. I'm more worried about you, Cash."

The happiness drains away when she mentions my legal issues, which aren't solved by any means. "What does your lawyer say? Does he think everything will be okay?"

I want to tell her the truth because I don't want her to think I'm simply a liar about everything, but this one topic will have to wait for honesty. She doesn't need to know things aren't going to be as easy for me as she wishes.

"My lawyer is one of those sharks you hear about, so I'm not worried. Everything will be fine. It's just going to take some time. But you're here, and that's all that matters, so why don't we move away from the front door of my brother's apartment and relax. We have hours to spend and catch up together."

As I guide her to the living room, she looks around at Alex's place and asks, "Is your brother here?"

I point toward the kitchen and say, "No, he's at work. Do you want anything to eat or drink? I think he's got some stuff in the refrigerator. I haven't exactly been eating much since I got here."

"No. I'm good. I just want to be with you. I don't care about anything else," she says sweetly while she searches out the couch.

Quickly, I grab the blanket I used to sleep with and toss it over on the chair on the other side of the room. "Sorry. I'm basically doing all of my living right here. Not exactly the way I want anyone to see me, especially you."

When she sits down, she grabs my hand to pull me down next to her. In her eyes, I see the kindness that's so much of who she is. I'm embarrassed because this isn't what I want her to think of me, but I don't have to be. She doesn't judge people like that.

"I don't care about where you sleep. All I care about is that I get to be with you, Cash."

"I know. It's just that this isn't anywhere as nice as your house. I don't want you to think you're slumming it with me because I'm basically homeless and sleeping on relatives' couches."

That makes her frown, and she lifts my hand to her lips to kiss my knuckles. "If you need somewhere to stay, you can come to my house. I don't care what my lawyer says. When someone you care about needs your help, you give it to them."

"I'm good here. Honest. My lawyer told me the same thing yours did. He took my phone so I wouldn't call you. I just couldn't stay away," I admit.

Savannah falls silent and looks away down at her hands in her lap. When she doesn't say anything for a long moment, I whisper, "What? Whatever it is, you can tell me. I'll understand."

She hesitates but finally says in a tiny voice, "I think I love you, Cash. I'm sorry. That's probably the last thing you need now."

How could she think hearing something so wonderful could ever be a bad thing, no matter when a man would hear it?

Gently, I turn her to face me and look into those soulful dark eyes staring up at me. "To know a woman like you loves me after everything that's happened? That's exactly what I need."

"Really? It doesn't add to your problems? I was

worried it might. I mean, we only went out a couple times and we've only slept together once. I thought maybe you'd think I was jumping the gun or being needy."

I shake my head and smile at how wrong she is about all of that. "You saying you love me could never be a problem, Savannah. I know we've been moving fast, but I feel like that's right for us. I love you too. These last few days have shown me that."

Her eyes fill with tears even as she gives me a big smile. "You do?"

"I do."

"That makes me so happy. I thought after the other night that I might never get the chance to tell you how I feel."

Dipping my head, I kiss her and love how gentle she is. "I'm the one who should be worried about you not wanting me to feel anything for you. I can't promise anything, Savannah. I don't know what's going to happen with the charges and the trial. You deserve someone who doesn't have all those problems when he says he loves you."

Savannah looks into my eyes and shakes her head. "I deserve someone who loves me. Nobody gets to choose what the circumstances are when you fall in love. That you love me and I love you is all that's important."

I wish that was the truth, but for tonight, maybe it can be.

CHAPTER TEN

ash

"So, where's your bedroom?" Savannah asks innocently and then looks shyly toward the hallway.

I smile, sensing where she's going with this but more than a little embarrassed about the true answer to that question. "You're sitting in it."

She focuses her gaze on me and bites her lip. "Oh. Okay. Then I guess us being together is impossible?"

Pulling her onto my lap, I slide my hands over her shoulders and draw her into a kiss that I hope shows her how much I want to be with her. "Nothing's impossible. Alex won't be home for hours, so we have the place all to ourselves. If you don't mind this couch, that is."

Smiling, she leans in toward me and sighs as she

presses her lips to mine. "I don't mind anything as long as I can be with you."

My hands run down her sides and come to rest on her hips straddling me. "I've missed you, Savannah."

She nods and begins lifting my shirt up over my head. "I missed you too, Cash. And I think I really like when you don't shave."

I smile, happy she likes my new look that came from not giving a damn about anything recently. Running my fingertips over it, I ask, "Not too scruffy?"

Savannah shakes her head and looks down at me with something sexy in her eyes. "Not at all. I like it. A lot."

With me half undressed, she runs her tongue across her lower lip. Stuffing my hand in her hair, I pull her mouth down to meet mine in a kiss I've waited days to give her. Our tongues slide over each other, teasing our need higher and higher. I'm hard as a rock with her still fully dressed in shorts and a t-shirt, and all I can think about is her naked riding my cock.

I start to undress her, eagerly pushing her dark blue t-shirt up over her head to reveal a black bra I've never seen before. It looks beautiful on her, and as I caress her skin just above the silky fabric, I smile.

"Is this new? All I've ever seen you in are white and pink."

Savannah nods and moves her hands around to her back to unhook it. "I've had it for a while. I told myself it would be good for when I wear dark clothes, but the truth is I bought it because it made me feel sexy."

As she slides the black silk straps down off her shoulders and tosses it onto the couch next to us, I silently think to myself that I prefer her naked just like she is now. I sense she's shy about the bra, though, so I pick it up off the couch and run my fingertips over the satin fabric.

"It's beautiful, just like the woman who was wearing it. I loved it on you."

With a giggle, she completes my unspoken thought. "But you love it better off me because you like to have me naked."

She blushes as I nod, and I cup her breasts in my hands, loving how they fit perfectly in my palms. "I'm not going to lie. I do love you naked for me, so why don't we get those shorts off you right now?"

"No foreplay tonight?" she asks, sliding her hands over my shoulders and leaving a trail of need on my skin in their wake.

"I'm struggling to hold back how much I want you already, and you've only been here for a few minutes," I admit before taking her nipple between my lips and giving it a gentle suck.

With a soft moan, she shows me she's having a hard time holding back too, even if she's afraid to admit it. Her fingers slide through my hair and tighten when I tenderly bite down on her hard nipple.

I look up to see pure need in her expression as she stares down at me. "You let me know how much foreplay you want, okay?"

The answer flashes in her eyes, and I know she's as ready for me as I am for her.

"That's enough. Are you sure your brother won't be walking through that door anytime soon?" she asks and then opens my belt before I give her an answer.

I lift her up off me and start to nudge her shorts over her hips. "He's gone until at least midnight, if not later. We're good."

At hearing that, she rolls off my lap onto the couch and shimmies out of her shorts and black panties that match the bra while I tug my pants and boxer briefs down my legs. We rush, desperate to feel one another again.

Savannah smiles when she sees me naked and climbs back on top of my lap. She rolls her hips, and her bare pussy presses against my hard cock, exciting me even more. I love how sweet and innocent she can be one minute and then sexy and full of abandon the next.

I look up at her and can't believe this incredible woman is here with me after all that's happened. With loving eyes, I watch her bite her lower lip and roll her hips again, adoring every tiny thing she does.

My hands teasing her breasts, I whisper, "You are so beautiful. You have no idea how happy I am that you came to me tonight, Savannah."

"Mmmm...I missed you so much, Cash. I wanted to see you before this..."

I stop her explanation with a long kiss that makes her moan softly into my mouth. She doesn't have to justify why we had to be apart. That wasn't because of anything she did. The fault lies entirely with me, and tonight, I want to make up for everything she's gone through in the past few days because of that.

Against that perfect mouth of hers, I say, "Shhh… it's okay. It was all my fault, Savannah. You don't need to say another word."

"I was so worried, Cash. I'm scared I'm going to lose you."

I shake my head and kiss her again to make her fears disappear. "It's going to be okay. I promise."

That's a lie, but at this moment when she sounds so terrified, I can't let her believe we're on borrowed time. I want tonight to be my chance to show her how much I care for her, not merely a few hours where I pretend, so I pull her to me and slide my cock between her wet folds.

She leans back and smiles before lifting herself up on her knees. With a roll of her hips, she slowly eases down onto my cock until I'm fully inside her. She's wet and tight and perfect in every way I could ever imagine.

I set my hands on her hips and press my fingertips into her skin to control how fast she rides me. If I could, I'd make this last forever, but since that's impossible, I'll take our lovemaking slow so I can enjoy every move of her hips, every time I slide into her tight cunt. There's no need to rush. We have hours before our night together must end.

"You're driving me crazy," Savannah whines sweetly when she tries to speed up and I won't let her. "I've been waiting for days, and now you're making me go in slow motion."

Looking up at her, I love how incredibly sexy she looks pouting about not letting her ride my cock the way she wants to. "I'm trying to draw things out so we get to enjoy ourselves."

"And I'm trying to come and you're stopping me."

God, I love that pout!

I release my hold on her hips and push my arms out to my sides. "I can't say no to you, so it's all yours. Let me see you ride me, baby."

She leans down and kisses me long and deep, rolling her hips to take every inch of me inside her. A tiny moan against my lips ends the kiss, and then she sits up straight and smiles down at me.

"You look so good sitting there. I worried I'd never get to see you like this again."

I hate the tinge of sadness in her voice, even as she fucks me, so I press my thumb against her clit and smile up at her as I gently rub circles against her. "No thinking about that now. You want to come, so let me see you come all over my cock."

Closing her eyes, she tilts her head back and says my name before she begins to ride me in earnest. My hands instinctively return to her hips, and with every time she bucks against me, I push her down hard to fill her completely. I watch the perfect woman ride me without hesitation or inhibition, her body rolling and her breasts bouncing up and down. There's no fear, no worry. Just exactly what the two of us need after too long away from one another.

I feel her body begin to tighten around me, and Savannah leans forward to kiss me. Our mouths crash against one another in desperation and utter need. Her teeth sink into my lip and she bites down as the very first moments of her orgasm roll through her.

She slides down on my cock one last time and stops, but her body trembles against me, squeezing me through her release. In my ear, she lets out a heavy sigh.

"Oh, God…I don't want to stop, but I don't know if I have an ounce of strength left in me."

I haven't come yet, so I whisper, "Hang on tight. I'll do the rest."

Cupping her ass in my hands, I pull her to me and pump my hips to fill her over and over. She's so fucking wet now after coming, and the slickness of her cunt only makes me more excited. I feel her fingernails dig into my shoulders and her hold on me tighten, and then she comes again with a squeal that sends my desire through the roof.

A second later, I still, my hands on her hips and pressing her down as my cock fills her with everything I have. Savannah collapses against me, our sweaty bodies pressing against one another so it's hard to tell where one of us begins and the other ends.

I listen to her soft breathing near my ear and then feel her turn her head. She presses a kiss to my neck and whispers, "I don't want to miss you again, Cash. I'm afraid that's what's going to happen, though."

"Don't worry about that now," I say, closing my eyes to force myself to sound positive about what's about to happen to me in the coming days. "All that matters is you're here with me now. That's all I care about."

She begins to say something, but the sound of something that sounds like the front door opening startles me. Before I can even look back, Savannah lets out a cry and hops off me onto the couch.

"Cash, I thought your brother wasn't going to be home for hours," she says, her voice full of pure terror as she scrambles to grab her clothes to cover herself.

"And here I thought I was coming home to cheer you up," Alex says with a chuckle. "Seems you found an even better way to lift your spirits."

CHAPTER ELEVEN

*S*avannah

I SQUEEZE MY EYES CLOSED TIGHTLY AND CLUTCH my clothes to my body in the hopes that I'm covering at least the most intimate parts of me in front of Cash's brother. The sound of a belt buckle knocking off the coffee table and then the rustle of fabric against skin tells me at least Cash is dressed enough for his brother's arrival.

I'm still naked and clinging to my clothing like some kind of refugee.

"Savannah, this is my brother Alex. Alex, Savannah. What the hell are you doing home so early? I thought you said you'd be gone until at least midnight."

"Kane let me go because he'd called in another chef to take my place tonight. He thought he was doing me a favor since he heard you're staying here with me. I figured I'd come right home with that beer I promised and cheer you up. You don't look like you need my help, though."

When Alex answers Cash's question, he sounds far away like he's in another room, so I cautiously open my eyes and look around to see Cash standing in front of me and his brother nowhere to be found. I quickly dress and sit back on the couch, still utterly mortified but at least fully clothed.

"Please tell him he can come back in, okay? I feel terrible enough. I'd hate it if he felt like he wasn't welcome in his own home."

Cash smiles down at me and grabs his shirt off the floor. "Don't worry about Alex. He's cool. In fact, he's probably the coolest person in my family. If we had to get walked in on by anyway, it's best that it was him."

I force a smile, but his explanation does nothing to make me feel better. Small consolation that his cool brother saw me buck naked instead of say his parents. Oh, God! Is there another word more intense than mortified? Because that's what I'd be if his mother or father walked in on us just now.

"Everyone presentable?" Alex asks as he strolls into the living room and looks over at me. Extending his hand, he smiles and says, "Hi, I'm Cash's brother. Sorry we had to meet that way."

I shake it and try to feel less than utterly embarrassed that the first time he ever saw me I was naked, on top of his brother after sex, and on his couch. "Hi, I'm Savannah. I'm so sorry about this."

He waves away my apology like nothing bothers him. "No worries. I didn't realize my brother had a guest. It's nice to meet you, Savannah."

Turning to look at Cash, he jokes, "Maybe we should have some kind of system where you leave a sign out that lets me know you're busy in here and I need to get lost. You know, since you don't have a bedroom like I do?"

"You mean like an actual sign that says something like 'Go away. I'm having sex' or something a little more subtle?" Cash asks and then laughs.

My cheeks heat up as a red-hot blush feels like it's searing my skin. I'm so not used to having people walk in on me while I'm having sex. True, I haven't been with a man for a while, so I'm not really used to anything concerning sex. All the same, having a grown man walk in while I'm naked and straddling someone is definitely not what I was expecting tonight.

"Savannah looks like she's about to die of embarrassment, so maybe we shouldn't be joking about this right now. Maybe a beer would make everyone feel better?" Alex offers before walking out to the kitchen.

Cash turns to look at me, and in his blue eyes, I see he's uncomfortable too. Taking my hand, he brings it to his lips in a kiss and whispers, "I had no idea he'd be back so early. Honest. If I did, I wouldn't have started anything."

How could I be upset when he's so sweet?

"It's okay. I just felt a bit exposed. Your brother

seems very nice, especially considering this is his home and he just caught us having sex on his couch."

"I told you. Alex is cool. Trust me. You don't have to feel bad at all about this."

His brother appears again from the kitchen and sets down a beer for each of us on the coffee table. "I got the kind you said you liked last time you were at Grandma's. It's ice cold, so it should taste great."

I look over at Cash as he grabs mine and hands it to me. "Grandma? I don't know why, but I didn't expect you to have a grandmother."

A smile lights up his face. "Oh, yeah. Our grandmother is kickass. Alexandria March, who Alex is named after, rules the family with a velvet hammer, right, Alex?"

His brother nods his head before taking a drink of beer. "Our grandmother is super cool but she doesn't take any shit from anyone. She's definitely not some hunched over little old lady. You cross Alexandria March, you'll have scars afterward. That's for sure."

The two of them talk about how one time their grandmother had to lay down the law with all of her grandsons, and to hear them tell the story, she's like a cross between a ninja and the Terminator. I watch as the two brothers discuss that time and I can't help but notice they look nothing alike.

When there's a lull in the conversation, I nudge Cash and ask, "Do you look like one parent and Alex looks like the other? Except for a few similar features like your mouths and the shape of your faces, you don't really look like you come from the same family."

From across the room, Alex laughs and Cash shrugs like this question is nothing new to them. "I look like the one side of the family. My father, named Cassian too, takes after his father with the dark hair and blue eyes. Our cousin Liam, one of Kane's sons, the guy who Alex mentioned when he was explaining why he's home early, he takes after that side of the family too."

"Don't forget Wilder, who isn't even actually blood related but has dark hair and the same kind of blue eyes you guys do too," Alex adds.

"Oh, yeah. So my father and his brother Kane both have the dark hair and blue eyes thing going. Same as their father. I have it and Liam has it from Kane, and then Kane and my aunt Abbi adopted a kid named Wilder and he strangely looks more like us than everyone on the other side of the family who looks like Alex."

As I work to untangle all of that information about the March family, Alex tries to clear things up by saying, "It's much simpler than Cash is making it. You either look like him or you look like me in the March family."

"So you don't look like your mother?" I ask, still confused.

Cash and Alex look at one another and both shrug. "Not really. She has brown eyes, but she's got red hair," Alex says. "You'd have to see our uncle Stefan, the youngest March brother, to know that I look like that side of the family. Grandma, Stefan, Cade, his son, and I all have the brown hair and brown eyes."

"Well, not Grandma anymore," Cash says with a laugh. "Now she's got no color in her hair at all. Still has the brown eyes, though."

"Our family is like a class in genetics."

"That's so interesting. My younger sister and I are convinced my mother had an affair with the mailman because we don't look a thing like our older brother and sister. They look like my father, but we don't look like either of our parents. Somewhere out there is a man delivering mail who probably looks just like us."

Alex laughs and raises his bottle of beer. "To genetics, the reason we look like we do."

Cash and I raise our bottles to toast genetics, and after we all take a drink, he looks over at me. "You aren't exaggerating. Cheyenne looks like you, but your older brother and sister look like they come from another family."

"Actually, I think Cheyenne and I look like we're from another family since we arrived last."

We fall silent for a few moments before Cash sits back on the couch and says, "You'd love her sister. She's all fire and sass. Obviously, she's beautiful too, but she's got a way about her that would keep you on your toes."

Alex smiles at his brother's attempt to get him interested in my sister. He doesn't look like he needs any help in the getting women department, though. Between his looks, his muscular body, and the tattoos, I imagine he doesn't spend too many nights alone like tonight.

"As you can tell, my brother thinks I need a

girlfriend. I'm sure your sister is great. I just wonder why everyone sees me as perfect for all their blind date set-ups," Alex says before taking another drink of beer.

"Who else is trying to set you up?" Cash asks like he's intensely curious about the answer.

With a shrug, Alex says, "Cade, mainly. I was hanging out with Hailey's friend Meadow there for a while, but things have cooled off. So now Cade suggests someone at least once every few days. I'm beginning to feel like a charity case here."

Cash turns to me and smiles. "This is the most I've heard my brother talk about the opposite sex since high school and Katie Connors."

"Well, that's because Savannah's here. If it was just the two of us sitting around drinking beers, there'd be long stretches of time where we said nothing punctuated by me busting your ass about something. Your girlfriend was uncomfortable enough when I walked in here, so I figured I'd be polite and talk instead of sitting here silent. And what the hell? Katie Connors. Talk about a blast from the past. I dated her in tenth grade, for God's sake. I think she's married with four kids now."

When Alex finishes, Cash nods at me like he knew he'd react that way. All I can think about is how he called me Cash's girlfriend. I am that, I guess. I hadn't thought about it that way, but I am.

Out of the blue, Alex stands up and asks, "Who's hungry? I'm starving, even though I barely worked for ten minutes tonight. I'm going to whip up something, so if you have any requests, make them now."

"I could go for something with pasta," Cash calls out as Alex heads toward the kitchen. "Savannah, anything you feel like you want?"

Shaking my head, I look at him with utter confusion. "Does he always just jump up and decide to cook you something like this?"

"Alex is a chef. It's who he is. He loves cooking, so I'm not surprised that the first time he's meeting you he wants to make you something. Trust me, whatever he makes, you're going to love. He's that good."

"I knew he was a chef since you told me, but I hate to think he feels obligated to cook something because I'm here. It's a night off for him. We should order something in so he doesn't have to bother."

From the kitchen, Alex yells out, "I heard the forbidden words, Cash. Tell her now she has to stay for what I'm cooking or I'll be offended."

My eyes open in horror that I've insulted his brother, but Cash quickly shakes his head and laughs. "He's just kidding. Well, not about the forbidden words. No ordering in when he decides to cook. He won't be offended if you don't want to eat, but I'm not lying when I say everything he makes is fantastic. I'll probably gain twenty pounds by the time I have to go back home."

"Okay. As long as he doesn't feel like he has to do this because I'm here. It's bad enough he had to walk in on us naked on his couch. I hope he doesn't think he needs to feed us too."

Cash leans in and kisses me sweetly. "He doesn't. He likes cooking. It's his passion. Think of it this way. Alex literally enjoys good food. It's a hedonist thing, I think."

"I bet he'd make some woman a wonderful boyfriend then. Women love when men cook for them."

"Hmmm...maybe your sister would like that? I imagine Cheyenne could get into his food obsession."

I can't help but laugh at how cute he is. "Are you really trying to set your brother up with my sister? You don't think that's a little weird."

Shaking his head, Cash shrugs. "No. I'm not saying we should force anything between them. Just that she might like him and he might like her."

"He is very good looking. You guys must come from very good genes, no matter which side of the family you take after," I say truthfully.

Behind Cash, Alex smiles at me. "I'm flattered, but don't let my brother get you wrapped up in his matchmaking. He's still coming off that business of his, so he thinks everyone needs someone."

"Dude, what's with being a creeper like that? I didn't even hear you walk into the room."

Alex rolls his eyes before turning to walk back into the kitchen. "You know, Cash, this is my house. It's not really creeping since it's my place."

Cash twists his face into a grimace, but I can't deny his brother's right. "He's got you there. Anyway, it's okay. Cheyenne probably isn't in a good place to be getting set up with anyone anyway. She found out her school is letting her go because of all the publicity about the escort business, so I doubt she'd be interested in starting anything with anyone."

His expression changes to sadness in a flash, and I hate that he's blaming himself for what's happened with Cheyenne. We all went into this with our eyes open. That her school is too provincial to admit that it's okay for a woman to go out with a man on her own terms instead of society's terms is what's wrong, not him.

"I'm sorry, Savannah. She's lost her job because of me. I don't know how you can even stand to be here with me knowing that."

He hangs his head, refusing to look at me, so I gently tilt it up so he has to face me. In his blue eyes, I see such unhappiness that I want to do anything to make that go away.

"It's not your fault, Cash. Cheyenne is a big girl, just like I am. It's not fair, but this is the way it is. I guess they want kindergarten teachers to be happily married or old maids. I doubt Cheyenne will ever fit into the categories they think are acceptable."

A tiny smile lifts the corners of his mouth, brightening his entire face. "She's pretty sassy for a kindergarten teacher. I never would have guessed she taught little kids."

"They love her too. It's her energy. When she finds something she loves to do, she's all in. I guess in that way she's like your brother with cooking. For her, it's kids. She loves teaching them. Too bad her school doesn't value that as much as it values her living a sexless life."

Cash lets out a heavy sigh as the scent of garlic begins to fill the room. "It isn't the sexless life they care about. I'd guess most of the people she works with aren't getting it as much as they want. It's all the publicity, and that's my fault. I'm sorry, Savannah."

I hug him to me, hoping to take some of his unhappiness away. "She'll be okay. She has a place to stay with me if she needs to watch her finances for a while, and I'm happy to give her whatever she needs. I wish I could do that for you too, Cash. I want to help, but I don't know how."

Shaking his head, he pulls away like I've said something to upset him. "I don't need you to do anything but be here with me tonight. Everything else is being taken care of. I don't want you to worry."

By the look in his eyes, I see it's no use to argue with him. He's a man who prefers to protect a woman, and as much as I love that, I wish I could do something to make all his problems go away. Then we could be happy and together without having this hang over our heads.

Alex pokes his head out from the kitchen and smiles at us. "Shrimp scampi will be ready in just a few minutes. It's an old standby, but I didn't want to go all wild on you the first time we meet. I've got grilled asparagus and some roasted tomatoes brushed with olive oil, and for my brother who loves to walk on the wild side, I have angel hair pasta."

When he disappears, I watch Cash's expression

lighten with a smile. "So you're Mr. Wild when it comes to pasta?" I tease.

"Yeah. It kills Alex to make something so pedestrian, but he'll do it for family. It smells great, doesn't it?"

I have to admit it does. "At first, I thought it was just the smell of garlic floating through the house, but now I'm getting a whiff of herbs and spices. It smells incredible!"

"That's my kid brother. He's got skills when it comes to cooking. Wait until you taste this," Cash says as he stands and takes me by the hand.

As I join him to walk into the kitchen, I say I can't wait, but I know I heard something darker and sadder when he complimented Alex. Whatever talent his brother may have, Cash has talents too.

It's just that the state of Florida and the U.S. government don't think too highly of those skills. That doesn't change the fact that he and his friend built up that business to the success it was when they were arrested.

If he can do that, then he can do anything he puts his mind to. Whatever that may be. I just pray to God he has the chance to and doesn't have to spend the next decade or two in prison for what he's done.

CHAPTER TWELVE

ash

WHEN I WALK BACK INTO THE KITCHEN AFTER promising Savannah I'll see her tomorrow, Alex is sitting feet up on a chair looking perfectly content with a beer. I swear to God my brother has some inner peace thing I've just never been able to find inside myself.

"Thanks for the meal. Your food never fails to impress," I say as I sit down across from him at the kitchen table.

He lifts his beer bottle and smiles. "Then my job is done here."

Alex is uncharacteristically quiet, especially after meeting one of my girlfriends. True, he's not usually the type of person to give his opinion about someone new without getting to know them a little first, but he seems odd right now.

Is it possible he didn't like Savannah? What's there not to like? She's gorgeous, kind, intelligent — everything I could want in a woman.

When the silence between us runs into a minute and then two, even after I grab a beer for myself, I finally can't hold off a second more from asking him what he thought of her. "So? How about Savannah?"

He lifts the bottle to his lips and slowly takes a sip of beer. I wait for him to answer my question, but he doesn't say a word. As the seconds tick by, I begin to wonder what the hell is going on with him.

Finally, he sets the bottle down onto the table and nods. "She's wonderful. I can definitely see why you'd want to be with her."

Something about the way he says that sounds off. Wonderful should be a compliment, but coming out of his mouth now it sounds anything but.

"Okay, she's wonderful. But? I feel like there's a but there somewhere. What I can't understand is why."

He takes another sip of his beer and sighs. "Okay, you want my honest opinion?"

That doesn't sound good at all, but I do want to know what my brother thinks of her. "Yeah."

"She's sweet. Like Georgia peaches from where her name comes from sweet. And she's crazy about you. I'm guessing you know that, though. The way she looks at you when you aren't paying attention is like she adores you, Cash. Sweet and adoring are definitely good things."

Again, when he stops talking, it sounds like there should be a but following the last word. Since he isn't saying it, I do.

"Okay, so sweet and adoring are good things. I agree wholeheartedly. But?"

Now he gives me a heavy sigh. Fuck! What the hell is going on here?

"Alex, why don't you try just saying what's on your mind, okay? Enough beating around the fucking bush. Obviously, there's something you don't like about her. Just tell me already."

He smiles, like any of this is goddamned funny. "There's nothing to not like about her, Cash. She's beautiful and sweet and she adores you like the sun rises out your belly button. The only but I can think of, and it seems like a big but, is should you be messing around with her now?"

And there it is. The truth I haven't wanted to admit to myself coming out of my brother's mouth as crystal clear as it can be. Do I have any right to be keeping Savannah around when I've got nothing but trouble looking at me for God only knows how long?

"I'm not messing around with her," I say before taking a gulp of beer. I think I want to be drunk. No, I think right now I want to get plastered so I don't have to think about any of the mess my life is in.

"Okay. I didn't mean to say you're using her. That's not what I think at all. I actually think you care about this woman. It's sort of interesting in a psychological study kind of way to watch you with her. When I said she adores you, I guess I should have followed that up with you adore her too. I don't think I've ever seen you like this with anyone. That last girlfriend you had, Emily? You never looked at her like I saw you looking at Savannah tonight."

When the hell did my brother get so insightful? Or maybe it's just obvious how I feel about Savannah and how I never felt that way with Emily or anyone else before.

"Yeah, well, I do. I'm crazy about her for all the reasons you've mentioned and a bunch more. What's so wrong with that?" I ask, cringing at the defensiveness in my voice.

Alex hesitates for a long moment and then nods. "I got a really strong feeling she's not the kind of woman who can tough it out if things get bad. That's all. She's got a delicate thing about her that might make it very hard for her to handle what's coming at you. Maybe I'm reading her wrong. Wouldn't be the first time. I'm not some all-knowing being here. I'm just telling you what I was picking up on when we were talking."

Hanging my head, I let out a heavy sigh, hating that I've been wondering the same thing. "She lost her husband after they were married for only a year or so. I'm not sure she's really good with dealing with hard stuff."

When Alex doesn't say anything, I add, "I know. I shouldn't be doing anything with her now that I've got nothing but problems. What do I have to offer her?"

I look up to see him smiling. "Normally, I'd say a

lot. I mean, you aren't some homeless guy, Cash. You're my brother, so I might be a bit biased. You'll come back from this whole shitshow. I know you will. Right now, though, everything's up in the air. Is this the best time to be making plans with Savannah?"

Even as I silently answer no to his question, what my brother doesn't know is that's all I have to cling to now. Everything else has been taken away from me. I have no business. I have no success to fall back on or build on. I have nothing except family and friends and Savannah.

"So you think I should break up with her?" I ask, hating each word as it passes my lips.

Shaking his head, he frowns. "I didn't say that. I can't tell you what to do, Cash. I just wonder what's going to happen if the worst happens."

My eyes open wide at his mention of the worst. He's talking jail time. Me, Cash March, in prison for God only knows how many years. Fuck. Maybe I have no right playing around with Savannah, no matter how much I care for her, when my future looks so bleak, or at the very least, uncertain.

"Talk about bad luck. I finally find a woman I truly want to be with, and the rest of my life fucks things up royally," I say quietly.

"You've always been lucky, though, Cash, so I wouldn't count yourself out yet. Wait for what your lawyer has to say about things. Give it a few days before you make any decisions. Just do what's right for her because someone so sweet doesn't deserve to lose a second man in her life."

I wish I could disagree with any of that, but I can't. Savannah deserves so much better than to have to see me hauled off to prison after watching her husband die. She's too good for that.

She's too good for me. At least the man I am now.

CHAPTER THIRTEEN

S avannah

MY HANDS SHAKE FROM NERVOUS ENERGY AS I WAIT for Cash to arrive. He said he'd be here by ten this morning, but my twentieth glance in the last five minutes tells me it's nearly ten-thirty.

Oh, God! What if something happened and the police have him? I have no number to call other than his brother's, but do I really want to pester him with what I hope is needless worry?

Cash is okay. He's simply a little late. Except he's never been late before. Not even once. If anything, he's someone who likes to be early.

Please, let him be okay. Don't let him be stuck in some jail cell on his way to God only knows where.

A sound at the hotel room door makes me jump up off the edge of the bed, and I hurry over to look out the peephole. It's him! I knew all my worrying was all for nothing.

I fling open the door and practically burst into tears when I see him standing there in the flesh. He looks as wonderful as he always does, and my emotions swirl around inside me, threatening to make me turn into a blubbering fool.

"You're okay. I was worried," I say as he leans in to kiss me.

Cash smiles, but I can tell it's forced. "I got tied up with Alex. I'm sorry. I didn't mean to make you worry."

I watch him walk past me into the hotel room and know something's wrong. He doesn't seem like himself today, but why?

By the time I sit down with him on the bed, fear fills me. He's heard from his lawyer, and it's bad news. Even more, he doesn't know how to tell me.

Taking his hand in mine, I bring it to my lips and kiss his knuckles. I look into his eyes and think I see the love he confessed for me last night, but there's something else there I don't like.

"Is everything okay, Cash?" I ask, struggling to keep my voice level.

He nods and gives me another forced smile. Why does he have to pretend to be happy now that he's here with me?

I wait for him to begin speaking, but he remains silent. I hate not hearing him say even a single syllable at this moment. I'm sure he has bad news to tell me.

"Did you sleep well? I can't imagine that couch is

as comfortable as a bed," I say, desperate to fill the empty space in what should be a conversation between us.

He shakes his head. "Not bad. It's better than a cot in a jail cell, so there's that."

Oh, God! Why did he mention jail? He definitely heard something from his lawyer, but he doesn't know how to tell me. I just want the truth. I can handle it if I know what's going on.

Standing, I drop his hand from mine and walk over to the window to look out over the water. "So is this how you are when you don't want to face up to reality? Because I have a sense you have something you want to say to me but you don't know how to."

I turn around and add, "All I want is the truth, Cash. I'm like everyone else in this world. Just give me the truth and I'll decide what I want to do from there."

His expression morphs from worried to stunned. He stares at me for a few moments, his blue eyes wide like he can't believe what I just said, but then he takes a deep breath in and nods.

Maybe now I'll get him to tell me what's going on.

"I wasn't trying to be mysterious or anything. I just don't know how to say what I have to say."

Every word sounds like it's being pulled from his throat, like he's practically choking on each one. Is it really as bad as I thought as my imagination ran away with me before he arrived?

"Just say it, Cash," I whisper, my voice trembling in fear.

He winces as if he's in pain, and I brace myself for the worst news of all. They have enough evidence to send him to jail. That's what he has to tell me.

Oh, God. I don't know if I can handle that truth.

Looking down at his hands, he finally says what's on his mind. "I don't think we should see each other anymore."

The words hit me like a slap to the face. My legs suddenly feel weak, so I reach out and grab the chair at the little table near the window. He doesn't want to see me anymore. Why is he saying this after he asked me to drive down here to see him and we spent last night together and had a wonderful time?

"What? Why?" I ask as tears threaten to drown out anything I might want to say.

"I just think it would be for the best," he says quietly, but I hear no emotion in his voice.

"That's not an answer why, Cash. I, at least, deserve to know why you're dumping me," I say, gripping the chair so I don't fall.

He shrugs, like this is nothing to him. "Things are just really crazy now. I think it would be for the best if we didn't see each other because of that."

Hurt courses through me, and even though I think I might collapse if I let go of my hold on that damn chair, I storm over to where he sits on the edge of the bed and stop in front of him. "Did you practice that a few times before you came here? Maybe that's why you were late? Try it out on your brother to see if it sounded genuine enough? Well, let me tell you it doesn't. It sounds like bullshit, Cash."

It takes a few seconds for my mini-rant to filter through his brain, but when he looks up at me, I can see he understands I'm angry about whatever he's trying to do. I also see he's surprised that little Savannah, the one who's always so sweet and kind all the time, is now standing here with her hands on her hips practically yelling at him.

Good. Maybe he needs to see this side of me. Not everyone gets to, but then again, not everyone makes me as angry as Cash has this morning.

"It's not bullshit, Savannah. It's the truth, and if you'd take a moment to think about it, you'd see it the same way."

I shake my head, refusing to buy that lame idea. "No. What I see is a man giving up. Is that what's happening? Are you giving up? I'm the one who should decide when things get too crazy for me to be around you because that's what this is, isn't it? Your attempt to protect me because you don't want to see me hurt? Because if not, then you aren't the man I thought you were, Cash March."

"You didn't even know my real name until a few days ago, Savannah. I haven't exactly been a great guy through all of this. I'm just trying to do what's right."

"Then I should be the one who gets to say you don't deserve me, not you. I accepted your apology for everything. Why do you think we can't work out now? What's happened to change your mind? Did you hear from your lawyer? Has something changed in the case?"

He merely shakes his head but doesn't answer. Why won't he tell me what's changed since last night?

"Did your brother say something to make you think we shouldn't be together? I thought we had a good time. Tell me the truth, Cash."

Suddenly, he leaps up off the bed and stands toe to toe with me. Staring into my eyes, he snaps, "I might be going to fucking jail, Savannah. I don't have anything to offer you now or any time in the near future. Fuck, I'm pretty much homeless since I can't go back to my apartment and I'm floating between my parents' house and my brother's place. Trust me, I'm not doing this because I'm a noble guy. It's just reality. You need to accept that."

His yelling startles me, and I feel myself begin to cry. I don't want to, though. He's not attacking me. He's attacking himself. I can see that, but why can't he?

I reach out for his hand and grab it, afraid if I don't keep him standing there with me that he'll leave and I'll never see him again. He turns away, refusing to face me, and I hate how ashamed he is of himself.

"Look at me, Cash."

He shakes his head and tries to pull his hand away, but I tighten my hold, unwilling to let go. I can't let things ends like this between us. No one has made me this happy in a long time, and I can't believe he can't say the same about me. What we have is too precious to let it slip away for anything, even the situation he's gotten himself into.

"Damnit, Cash. Look at me!"

Still, he won't, so I step in front of his face so he has to see me when I say what I have to say. His expression is filled with anguish, and those blue eyes I love look like they'll never show happiness again. God, I hate that.

"Cash, please listen to me. I think you are trying to do the noble thing when it comes to me, but I don't need you to do that. I love you knowing all the bad things yet still I want to be with you. Doesn't that count for anything? Don't I have a say in the matter of whether or not we stay together?"

He hangs his head and sighs. "Do you plan on saying this all the way up to the moment they drag me off to jail, Savannah?"

I fight to stop the tears filling my eyes at the thought of him being taken away like that. Swallowing hard, I say, "I plan on saying this until you get it through your head that I love you."

"Well, maybe you shouldn't," he snaps and then yanks his hand from my hold.

Walking across the room, he stands with his back to me staring out the window. I feel like even though there are only a few feet separating us, it's as if he's a million miles away and a wall is growing between us with every angry word we utter. I can't let him throw everything we are to one another away like this.

"You don't really believe that. I know you don't. Of course, I should love you. Why shouldn't I?"

The words barely hit the air before he spins around and yells, "Because I'm probably going to fucking prison, Savannah! What don't you understand about that?"

"Stop yelling at me! I'm not the one who put you into this position. Why are you attacking me like I've done something wrong?"

That sets him off, and he storms toward me with rage in his eyes. "No, I'm the one who put me in this position. I'm the one who put you in your position and your sister in her position, or more correctly, out of her position as a teacher because of the nightmare I've created. Since I'm the one who made this all happen, I get to be the one to say that I can't be with you anymore. Take it as a gift of fate, Savannah. Get out while you still can."

I push against his chest and scream, "I don't want to get out! Why won't you understand that?"

"Because I don't think you're a fool, but you're acting like one right now. When a man tells you he can't see you anymore, take him at his word. Trust me. There's no nobility here. Just a man who's about to be the newest inmate in the Florida state prison system."

"Stop saying that!" I exclaim, tired of hearing him refer to himself like that. "What happened? Did you hear from your attorney? What did he say?"

Cash shakes his head. "No. I just realized that it's not fair for me to string you along if the end of this road for us means waving goodbye as they take me to jail."

His continual insistence on acting like I'm not an adult who can make up her own mind makes something inside my brain snap. I ball my hands into tight fists and hit his chest and then I hit it again and again. Cash doesn't try to stop me or even hold my hands as I begin to sob and pummel him like a madwoman.

"You aren't that, Cash March!" I cry out. "And I'm not being strung along or a fool. I love you. That's worth dealing with anything that comes with you."

Finally, he wraps his fingers around my wrists and holds my hands in between us to stop me. "You're going to hurt yourself, so no more."

I look up into his eyes and see that same sadness as before. "Then you better not even think about letting my hands go because if you do, I'm just going to hit you again until I make you see that you aren't that man you keep saying you are."

"You're wrong. I'm exactly that man and worse."

"I don't care."

When the words hit my ears, I know I sound like an insolent little girl getting ready to stomp her feet. Too bad. If that's what it takes to make him see he's wrong, then I'll do that and more.

"In fact, I don't want to talk about this anymore. I woke up with one thought on my mind this morning, and even though you've done your damnedest to ruin the past half hour, I'm not going to let you."

With that, I begin to unbutton his pants as he stares down at me in shock. "What are you doing?"

I reach in and palm his cock, smiling up at him. "I'm not sure what happened between last night and today, but even if something wormed its way into your brain and made you forget everything you feel for me, I doubt you've forgotten the word for what I'm doing right now and what I plan to do in a minute."

"Nothing wormed into my brain, and yes, I still remember this and how much I like it, especially when it's with you. This doesn't change anything, though, Savannah."

Pushing him back onto the bed, I smile as he lays there looking up at me like I've lost my mind. "Sex doesn't have to be life-changing, Cash."

When I tug his pants down his legs and crawl on top of him, I lift my skirt to reveal just what I had planned for this morning that he almost ruined. Cash smiles and shakes his head.

"Has nothing I've said for the past thirty minutes gotten through to you?"

I lean down to kiss him before sliding my wet pussy the length of his cock. "No. Sorry. I was thinking of this the whole time and wasn't listening to a word you said."

Rolling my hips, I take every delicious inch of him inside me and sigh. Now that's what this morning was supposed to be. Pure satisfaction. No yelling. No nonsense about him going to jail. We don't need any more of that kind of talk.

Cash sets his hands on my hips and begins to move me up and down on him. He feels so fucking good, and all I want to do is go fast, but he insists on keeping my pace slow.

"I swear, you are the most difficult man in the world, Cash March. A woman says she loves you and then seduces you, and what is her reward? You won't give her what she wants."

He smiles and sits up to kiss me as I ride him. "You know I like to slow you down to prolong the pleasure."

As I wrap my arms around his neck and spread my legs wider to accommodate him, I smile. "What I know is after what you just put me through, you should be willing to give me ten orgasms just to make up for it."

Cash buries his hand in my hair and tugs hard while he kisses my neck. He's wild and uninhibited, and I love how his mouth on me and his cock inside me makes me want to scream in pure pleasure.

Against my skin, he moans, "Ten it is, then. You sure you're up for it?"

I tilt his head back and nod as I feel my first release begin to uncoil inside me. "I'm up for everything and anything with you, Cash. Never forget that."

His mouth devours mine, and a few moments later, I come hard on his cock like I know he wants me to. He tears at my shirt to get to my breasts, nipping my tender skin just above my bra. This is the man I love, the man I would give anything to have in my life.

He won't listen to reason, and he won't be swayed by my anger or my sadness. I won't lose him like I lost my husband. I couldn't do anything about cancer ravaging his body, but I can do something about Cash's problems.

And after I recover from what I plan to be a day full of sex with him, I intend on doing whatever I can to help him. He thinks I'm some delicate flower he might hurt because of what he's brought into my life, but he has no idea how strong I can be.

I'm not even sure I knew until all of this happened with him. I do now, though, and the world is about to find out what Savannah Gardener is like when the man she loves is in trouble.

ash

My father and I sit in the living room of my parents' house as we listen to my attorney give us an update on my case. So far, not much has changed, which for Correlli seems to be a good thing. For me, all I can think is no news isn't good news but a sign the cops are still digging into everything they can to get me.

"So that's about it. Everything's on hold for now, but don't interpret that as a negative. If they had all they need to announce even more charges, they'd do it. Hell, if they do, they'll hold a press conference for this kind of case. That they haven't says good things to me."

"Okay," I mumble, probably barely loud enough for him to hear even on a speakerphone. "Thanks."

"Cassian, I'll let you know if I hear anything and you can relay the information to Cash there, okay?"

"Thanks, Andrew. I appreciate it. Cash does too. We all do."

"My pleasure. Oh, Cash, you've been following what I told you to do, right? No contacting anyone associated with the escort service," Correlli says almost as if he wants to gently remind me of the singular rule he laid down.

The one I've broken over and over in the past few days since Savannah came to see me at Alex's three nights ago.

"Yeah. To the letter," I lie, hoping I sound more convincing to his ears than I do to mine.

Correlli hesitates for a moment before he speaks again. "Good! Stay strong and don't let yourself get down. We're still in the early stages of this game, Cash."

I want to ask if I can go back to my apartment any time soon, but now doesn't seem to be a good time. I'm not sure I could sound convincing if he asked me why I want to go home. I'd probably sound like a lovesick puppy if he pressed me for a real answer.

"Okay, well then, I'll call if I hear anything. Remember, silence isn't bad, so focus on that. Talk to you later."

With that, my attorney ends the call and I sit there in my parents' living room wondering if I'll ever get to have a life again. A real life, like a grown man should have, not the lame version of a life where I have to stay with my younger brother or my parents and can't speak to the one person who makes me happier than any other soul in the world.

My father stands up, pulling me out of my thoughts about Savannah. "I'm heading to the restaurant today. Kane thinks there won't be any issues since the media has gone from the parking lot. I'm pretty much losing my mind tinkering with things around here, and your mother might be planning to kill me since I've been underfoot for so long."

I move to leave with him, sure there's no reason for me to stay. "Okay. I'll walk out with you. I think Alex said he's working late tonight, so he's probably still home. He and I can hang out and I can pester him for another day."

That's meant as a joke, but my father doesn't even crack a smile. In fact, he doesn't seem to be paying attention to anything I'm saying at all, instead practically looking through me as I speak.

"Dad? Earth to Dad? You in there?" I ask and then follow his gaze to where he's focused behind me.

On my mother staring at the two of us with that ever-present look of sadness in her eyes.

"Cassian, are you leaving?"

He nods and gives her a tiny smile. "Yes, so you're finally rid of me, at least for the next few hours."

Her focus shifts to me exclusively. "Good. I want to talk to Cash."

"Sounds good. Cash, I'll call you later. Olivia, I'll let you know what time I'll be home, okay?" my father says as he makes a beeline for the door, obviously eager to get the hell out before my mother begins to say what's on her mind.

What she's been holding back for a week.

He leaves us standing there in the living room where Alex and I played as boys and I spent sick days home from school on the couch we used to have with the big puffy cushions that were perfect for laying your head on when you didn't feel good. Right now, I don't feel great as I wait for her to start talking. I figure it's her house and she's the one who's got some things on her mind, so better for everyone involved if I just keep my mouth shut and listen.

"Sit down, Cash. I need to get this off my chest so I don't have to walk around feeling so terrible anymore whenever I think of my son."

A rougher start than my mother's usual, but definitely not as bad as I expected for what I've done.

We sit down, me on the couch and my mother in her favorite grey and white striped chair that nobody thinks is comfortable but her. Dressed in a light blue dress, she leans back and crosses her legs, silent after that beginning statement.

I try to remember that my father, the person who knows her best in this world, believed she needed time and once she had that, things would turn out fine. They did for him when he screwed up that time when they were dating, so they'll be okay now too.

At least that's what I keep repeating to myself as one minute of silence stretches into two and three. She doesn't look at me, instead focusing on the window directly in front of her. I take a deep breath in and let it out until there isn't a hint of air in my lungs as I begin to wonder what she'll say next.

Will it be that I'm a complete and utter disappointment now that she knows I dropped out of law school? Will it be that I'm an embarrassment to the family for running an escort service and being arrested? Or will it be that she can never forgive me for lying to her all that time?

I get a pain in the pit of my stomach when I think of that last option. While I might not be best friends with my mother, she's the woman who gave birth to me. She took care of me when I had the flu and stood up for me when teachers said I was lazy. The idea of my mother cutting me out of her life because she can't bring herself to forgive me for the stupid things I've done makes me feel hollow inside.

As all of this runs through my head, she turns her body to face me, a sign she's ready to tell me what she wants to say. I smile, hoping that might blunt the rage I suspect will come at me at any moment.

But it isn't anger in her voice when she finally begins to speak. It's the thing that hurts more than anything else.

Sadness.

It's in her eyes and in her very posture, and now it covers every word she says after all these days of silence.

"I want to tell you a story. Your father and I have never told you or your brother about this, and we made everyone else in the family swear to never say a thing to you boys. The day your father and I were set to get married, I left him at the altar. I ran away, leaving him standing there at your grandmother's house. He was heartbroken, but I did it because I had found out right before our wedding day that I likely would never be able to have children. Your father was never shy about how he wanted a big family, and the idea that I'd be stealing that from him tore me up inside. So I ran away without telling him the truth and planned to never see him again, thinking that he'd be better off with someone else who could give him those kids that were so important to him."

I listen to her in shock since I've never heard this story. I've heard that the doctors thought my parents might have trouble having kids, but I didn't know it made her abandon their wedding.

She stops talking for a moment and takes a deep breath as a look of anguish comes over her. I have no idea what she's about to say, but whatever it is, it's hurting her right now.

"When I found out I was pregnant with you, Cash, it was the happiest moment of my life. Hands down the happiest moment. I love your father with all my heart, but until that day when I was sitting in my obstetrician's office and she said those wonderful words, 'Olivia, you're pregnant,' I had never felt that happy in my entire life. You were my miracle. I adored you from that moment on."

Hanging my head, I say barely loud enough for her to hear, "I'm so sorry, Mom."

She falls silent, and when I look up, tears are in

her eyes. Tears I put in her beautiful brown eyes that have always looked at me with such love.

I begin to say something, but she holds her hand up and shakes her head. "Please, let me finish. I promised myself I'd get through this without crying, and right now, that's not looking like a promise I'm going to get to keep. I just want to say this so you know why I couldn't talk to you this past week."

With a smile, I nod and wait for her to continue.

She wipes under her eyes and begins again. "You and Alex have been my miracle babies and what I'm most proud of in my life, but it's different with him. Maybe it's because he's a different kind of person. Maybe it's because he came second. I don't know. When you graduated from college and decided to go to law school, I couldn't tell enough people. I was so proud. Cash is going to be a lawyer. It seemed so right. Someone as smart and driven as you could do anything, so why not?"

When she stops speaking to wipe a few tears that have begun rolling down her cheeks, I can't stop myself from explaining why I couldn't be that person. "Mom, I'm sorry I didn't tell you that I hated law school. I know I should have, but I didn't want to disappoint everyone. You were so happy and Dad was so happy. I didn't want to face you and tell you I wasn't happy."

My mother nods, and she can't stop herself from crying now. "I know, honey, and I hate to think that you were that miserable ever in your life and you couldn't tell your father or me. I never wanted you to think that you had to do something that made you so unhappy simply to make us proud. I'll always be proud of you, Cash. I don't care what anyone says about what you've done. You're my miracle. From the moment you came into this world, I've been proud of you. That's never stopped, honey, and if you thought it did, I'm sorry for that. I never meant to make you think you don't make me proud every single day just by being you."

Damn. I expected her to lay into me for lying to her and then ream me out for getting arrested. I think I could have handled that. This is killing me. Now she's apologizing to me because she thinks she made me feel bad.

"Mom, don't. You did nothing wrong. Don't beat yourself up because I thought you weren't proud of me. You have every right to be angry and disappointed. I got arrested. I brought those media vultures to your home. I wouldn't blame you if you weren't proud of me now. I'm not proud of what I've done. Between the lying and the breaking the law, I didn't act like the person I pretended I was to everyone, but especially to you. For that, I'm sorry. You deserved better than my lying all this time. Everyone deserved better, but most of all, you."

Standing, I walk over to where she sits. "I'm so sorry, Mom. I never meant for all of this to happen. I know that's not much consolation now, but it's the truth. I promise."

She stands up, and through her tears, smiles up at me. Her hands cradle my face like when I was a little boy and something upset me. "I love you, Cash. I might not like anything I've found out you've done recently, but I'll always love you. Never forget that. And never forget that no matter what, you can always come to your father and me if you're ever in trouble. We're your parents. We've loved you before you were even born."

I wrap my arms around her and hug her as relief washes over me. "Thank you, Mom. I promise I will."

We stand there holding each other, and she lets out a heavy sigh against my shoulder. "That's all I ask."

Stepping back, she wipes her tear-stained face and smiles. "Call your brother and I'll call your father. I want the four of us to do something as a family today."

"Okay, Mom. Whatever you want."

It's the least I can do for the woman who gave birth to me, stood by me all my life, and now forgives me for the mess I've made of everything. Maybe it can be like when Alex and I were small and the four of us would watch a movie together on one Sunday a month. That could be nice. It would also give me a chance to tell them about Savannah.

CHAPTER FIFTEEN

ash

ALEX AND I SIT ON OPPOSITE ENDS OF THE COUCH as my mother buzzes around the room setting out bowls of popcorn. She always makes the best popcorn in the world. I don't know what she does to it, but it's lighter than air, even though it's drenched with butter.

We both grab our own bowls and begin devouring the snack, and my father sits down in the chair near the window and Alex. My brother tosses a few kernels up into the air before catching them in his mouth, a trick he's been able to do since he was a kid and one I've never been able to master.

When two pieces of popcorn fall onto my lap, Alex tosses a handful at me and laughs. "You still can't do that. Amazing."

Before I can respond to his insult, my mother sits

down in her chair and scolds the two of us. "Stop making a mess. Who got all the popcorn in the couch cushions?"

Alex quickly answers, laughing. "Cash, of course. He still can't throw a kernel of popcorn into the air and catch it in his mouth."

"That's not where your brother's talents lie."

Still chuckling, Alex asks, "Are we at the place where we can joke about what's happened? Because I have a great comeback for where his talents lie."

I look down at my bowl and shake my head. "Too soon, man. Too soon."

"No, we are not at that place, Alexander," my mother answers sharply. "That's going to take me a little more time, so no more talk about that today."

Glancing over at my brother, I whisper, "Alexander. She used your full name. Now you're in trouble."

I get a handful of popcorn thrown at me for that crack.

"So what are we watching?" my father asks, sounding like he's eager to move on from my brother's mistake.

"I saw a movie advertised the other day that sounded good," my mother says. "I can't remember the title, though. I think it was some kind of action film, so that would make all of us happy. Go to the search thing and look for something with that really tall guy who's in all those action movies."

My father, Alex, and I look at each other, and it's obvious none of us have any idea what she's talking about. Grabbing the remote, my father says into it, "Tall guy in action movies."

As we laugh at his effort to show how silly that sounds, he adds, "Try Abraham Lincoln."

I see out of the corner of my eye my mother scowl at him. "Not funny, Cassian."

"Why? He was tall. Or was he just tall because he wore that hat all the time?"

Alex leans over and whispers, "We're never going to watch anything with these two in charge. Someone needs to make an executive decision."

Reaching over toward my father, he grabs the remote from his hands. "Looks like it's going to have to be me. Let's get to the search section so at least we can see what we can choose from."

My brother navigates the TV to where our choices come up on the screen, but before he can start to highlight what's offered, I hear a familiar soft voice begin to speak. It only takes a second for me to realize it's Savannah, but what the hell would she be doing on TV?

Alex knows it's her too and turns to look at me. "Is that who I think it is?"

I snatch the remote out of his hand and get rid of that search screen to see her sitting with some woman with short black hair on the patio out near the pool at her house. The woman is talking about who Savannah is and who her husband was in the business world.

"Why are we watching this woman doing some interview?" my father asks, but my attention is glued to the scene in front of me on the TV.

The dark haired interviewer listens to something Savannah says about wanting to tell the whole truth, and my heart feels like it's stuck in my throat. Jesus Christ, what is she planning to tell the truth about?

A singular thought repeats on a loop in my head. Don't do this, Savannah. Don't tell them about us.

It feels like all the air has been sucked out of the room around me. I hang on every word she says, praying to God she isn't doing what I think she's doing. Why she would think this would be a good idea I can't fathom.

"Who is this woman?" my mother asks, looking around for someone to explain what the hell we're doing watching this interview.

"It's Savannah Gardener, the wife of Carson Gardener," my father says, and I snap my head to the left to stare at him. How does he know?

"Oh, the man who owned those hotels you and Kane were in talks with to get CK into some of his locations a while back. I thought you said he was our age. She looks more like Alex's age to me."

Beside me, my brother says, "Wasn't he some billionaire hotel guy?" and for a moment, I can't tell if he's asking everyone that question or just me.

I look over and nod, unsure what's about to happen on the TV but hating what's going on right here in this room. "Yeah."

And then he says the words that make the room fall silent. "That's Cash's girlfriend, by the way."

By the way? By the fucking way? Thanks for dropping that bombshell into the mix right as we wait to hear what she's about to tell this local news reporter.

Finally, after what seems like an eternity, my father asks, "You're dating Carson Gardener's wife?"

I quickly correct his mistake, hoping at least that will make whatever happens next less painful. "Widow. Her husband died of cancer a couple years back."

Three sets of eyes focus on me, but all I can focus on is Savannah on the TV as the interviewer asks a question that sounds so incredible I can't believe my ears. Holy fuck! She didn't just ask what she knows about me and the escort service.

Savannah smiles sweetly, definitely not the way she should when she talks about this, and tilts her head to the side like she sees something she likes. I'm sure at any minute the floor is going to open up and swallow me as my family acts like they're watching a tennis match, their heads moving as they first look at me and then look at the TV and then back at me again.

"Shayla, it's been so wrong of the press and the authorities to lay all of this at Cash and Damon's doorstep. I had a part in it too, and I'm not getting any of the blame. Yes, I know I look young and innocent, but I'm just as guilty here."

My mouth drops open as the three people around me whip their heads around to stare in my direction. I have no idea where's Savannah's going with this, so I can't help them with any answers.

"So are you saying that you were involved in running the business with Cassian March IV and

Damon Childress?" the interviewer Shayla asks, leaning forward in her chair like she wants to be as close as possible to Savannah when she gives her answer.

And then she does the unthinkable.

Nodding, she smiles sweetly again and says, "Yes. I mean, you can't think two law school dropouts would have the capital to start up a business like that, now do you? That takes money. I was the money part, a silent partner but a partner nonetheless. I bankrolled the business, Shayla."

Fuck. Why would she say that? What is she thinking by lying about this?

I try to take a full breath of air in, but it's like I'm trapped in a vacuum and there's not an ounce of oxygen in my parents' living room. My family continues to stare at me, stunned by what they're hearing and no doubt looking for some answers from me.

But I have none.

My father's phone ringing breaks the silence, and he answers it with, "Andrew, he's right here, and I don't think he knows what's going on either."

He sets his phone on the table in between the chairs and couch, and a second later, my attorney says, "So you have no idea what the hell this woman is talking about?"

I can barely find the ability to talk, much less give him an answer that will make him happy about what's going on with this interview. Looking up at the TV, I watch Savannah as she continues to dig a hole deeper for herself, completely unsure why she's doing this.

"No. I know Savannah. I've been dating her for the past month. She would never hurt a soul. She's probably thinking by some twisted logic this will help me. She had no part in running the business, and she certainly didn't bankroll it. She was a client, and she used an escort once toward the end."

"Well, I better damn well know what the hell his name is because together, they're liable to open a whole new can of worms I want to know about before it gets dumped in my lap," Correlli barks.

And for yet another time in all of this, I wish I had never started this whole thing with Damon. Quietly, I admit the truth of who Savannah's escort is.

"It was me. I was the one who did the job."

For a second, I can't hear a thing because my heartbeat is pounding so loudly in my ears. Thankfully, Correlli needs that time to process my answer before he says, "But you told me you didn't do the work. You just managed the company."

Christ, having to talk about this in front of my entire family is pure fucking agony.

"I didn't. Not after the first few months when we had enough guys working for us. She wanted an escort over Labor Day weekend, and none of my guys could do it, so I went on the job. I took her to her brother's wedding. Nothing big. We had a nice time."

He doesn't need to know that—no one does—but I feel like I need to say that so she doesn't sound like some sad, desperate soul who couldn't find a date, and

I don't sound like some fucking predator like they're making us out to be in the press.

"So any idea why she's spinning this tale? Because she sounds pretty damn convincing to me. I'm guessing Shayla's audience is eating it up."

I glance around at my parents and my brother, who look like they're waited with bated breath to know the answer to that question. "No. She probably just wants to help."

"Well, it's going to get her neck-deep in trouble. Wait a second. You said you've been dating her. Did you have any contact with her since I took your phone off you and told you to stay away with anyone connected to the business?" Correlli asks in a voice that sounds like he wants to come right through the phone and shake the hell out of me.

"Yeah."

I guess I could explain more, but what's the point? He asked. I answered. No reason to lie now.

"You didn't tell her to do this, did you, Cash?"

"No! I would never do that," I answer as I glance up at the screen to look at Savannah's beautiful face. "I don't want her anywhere near any of this. She's too good, and she's completely innocent. She had nothing to do with Damon or me running the business."

A sound like a groan of disgust comes through the phone, but then when he starts talking again, Correlli doesn't sound as upset as he did a few moments ago. "Well, I'm going to use this to any advantage I can, Cash. As your attorney, if I see a door open, I'm walking through. If I can cast doubt on any of what the police think by throwing this woman into the mix, I'll do it."

Jesus, just the thought of her being used like that makes me feel like someone's ripping my heart out. I don't want Savannah in the middle of this. She doesn't deserve that, no matter how much she's trying to help me.

"Andrew, leave her out of everything. She's not part of this. If they have the evidence to come after me, then that's what has to happen. Savannah isn't part of some game plan I'll use when things get tough. Leave her be."

"As you wish, but fair warning. Your co-owner's attorney is going to go hard with her, if he can use her. We should too. If she's truly not involved, then she won't be in danger, but it will allow us to cast doubt on anything the prosecution might have down the road."

I shake my head but say nothing. I know what his job is, but my responsibility as the man who loves Savannah is to protect her. Those two things aren't compatible.

My father grabs his phone from the coffee table and takes the attorney off speakerphone. "Andrew, we understand and appreciate all you're doing to help Cash. Do what you must."

The four of us sit in silence as Savannah's interview ends and she gives one final sweet smile to the woman sitting in front of her. I'll never be able to forgive myself if anything happens to her because of this.

Finally, my mother leans over and gives my arm a gentle squeeze. "She's just beautiful, Cash."

I look at her and smile at her attempt to make things better for me after all I've done. "She is. And sweet and kind and obviously out of her mind."

"Oh, honey. She's not crazy. She's in love with you. That's why she did that. I hope we get the chance to meet her someday because any woman that in love with one of my boys is someone I want to know."

"Thanks, Mom. I hope you do get to meet her someday."

Assuming I'm not in prison and the authorities haven't taken every last dime Savannah has to her name because they think she was running an illegal escort service.

God, I need to talk to her. She has to know as much as I love what she's trying to do, I can't let her take the blame for my mistakes.

No matter how much she loves me or I love her.

CHAPTER SIXTEEN

$\mathcal{S}$avannah

CHEYENNE STANDS IN THE DOORWAY AS SHAYLA AND her crew leave one by one through the house. The interview went even better than I anticipated. Never one to be on camera, I swallowed my pride and did what I had to do.

Now I can only hope it will help Cash.

When the last of them leave, my sister turns to me and shakes her head. "You have balls the size of Texas and I swear to God they're brass. If I didn't know the facts, I'd think every word you said to that woman was the honest to God truth. You must be more in love with that man than I ever could be with anyone to do what you just did."

My sister's admiration makes me smile, but it didn't take bravery to do that. Well, other than working up the courage to be seen on TV. All it took was knowing that I want to help Cash in any way I can.

"I do love him, which is why I couldn't just sit around waiting for things to happen to him. Now, maybe they'll get distracted and pay attention to me for a while. I can afford it. Robert will probably be calling any minute to have a conniption, but since I had no real part in the escort business and it won't take the police long to figure that out, I'll be fine. I'm just hoping it makes the case against Cash weaker. If that happens, then maybe his lawyer can get the charges dropped or lessened to misdemeanors that he won't have to do jail time for."

Cheyenne shakes her head again and smiles. "Ballsy and smart with money to burn. In my next life, I'd like to come back as you, please."

When she walks back into the house, I think to myself that I can only hope all three of those things are true about me. The money isn't in dispute, but ballsy and smart? I guess I'll have to see.

My lawyer must have had to get CPR after hearing about the interview because he doesn't call for nearly ninety minutes. When he does, though, he's as out of his mind as I imagined he would be when I contacted Shayla at the station and offered her an exclusive interview.

"Are you insane? Please just answer that for me. Are you?" he asks, his voice frantic.

I don't think I've ever heard Robert sound like this. "No, I'm not insane."

"Didn't you hear me when I said not to contact him? I heard me say it. Did you?"

"Yes."

Instead of frustrating him further, my simple answers seem to take all the energy out of him. "You can't lie like that, Savannah," he says in his best scolding voice but far calmer now.

"Of course, you can. People lie to the press all the time. That's something you tell children. We're adults, Robert. We know better."

I sound pretty damn cavalier for someone who's just opened Pandora's Box. I'm not as calm as I seem, especially since I haven't heard from Cash yet. He has to have heard about what I did by now.

"Well, you can't lie to the police then."

He can't see me shrug before I answer, "I had no intention of lying to the police. I know what not to do. I'm not an idiot."

Robert makes a tsk-tsk sound before saying, "When I heard about this craziness, all I could think was what Carson would have to say about you doing this, Savannah. This isn't like you, and I don't think he'd be happy."

I've had enough scolding from a man I'm not sleeping with for one day, so I snap back, "Are we talking about Carson Gardener, a man who routinely lied to the press and anyone else in the public if he thought it would help his business? The man who walked the finest of lines when it came to telling the truth, even to government officials, particularly in foreign countries? That Carson Gardener, Robert?"

He's left speechless, so I continue to remind him of some facts he clearly has chosen to forget. "My dearly departed husband was the one who schooled me on when to be absolutely truthful and when you can abandon that for what benefits you. He knew, like you do, that a person should always be truthful to the ones they love and their attorneys. Everyone else, feel free to fudge the truth as much as you can get away with. So please don't lecture me on what Carson would think of what I did today."

Robert grunts like he's thoroughly disgusted, but he knows I'm right. He's just not used to me acting this way. No one is. Too bad. They better get used to it because I'm tired of sitting in my house afraid to take a chance on life.

Some things are worth fighting for. Some people are worth taking whatever risks necessary for. This is the new Savannah. Live with it.

"If the police come to the house, don't talk to them. Call me and I'll come over. Please tell me you'll at least do that."

He's practically begging, but he doesn't have to. I never had any intention of interacting with the police without an attorney present. I'm not an idiot.

"I promise, Robert. Don't worry. This will all be fine. You're forgetting one important thing I have going for me. I'm a wealthy woman. When was the last time you saw the cops make one of us do a perp walk?"

Another groan and then he asks, "Does the name Martha Stewart ring a bell?"

"They got her on insider trading. All I did was lead them on a wild goose chase. Not the same thing at all. Don't worry. It will all be fine. I'll call you if they show up. Until then, let me know if you hear anything, okay?"

He mumbles something about being an officer of the court and having to tell the truth before saying goodbye. I don't know what he's getting so upset about. Nobody asked him to lie about anything.

As I set my phone on the table next to me and close my eyes to enjoy the warm September day, I can't help but wonder why Cash hasn't contacted me today. He knows what I did. I'm sure of it. So why hasn't he called even once.

I don't know how long I sit there thinking of him, but Cheyenne interrupts my daydreaming when she clears her throat. Opening my eyes, I look over toward the doorway and see her standing there with Cash. Dressed in jeans and a black t-shirt, he's a sight for sore eyes.

With a smile, she says, "I'll leave you two alone."

It only takes a few seconds of him staring down at me to see the worry in his blue eyes. Or is he upset? That would explain why he drove two hours here to talk to me in person.

"What did you do, Savannah?"

"I did the only thing I could do, Cash. I couldn't let you be sent away. Not if I could stop that. So I interjected something new into the case."

He walks over to where I sit and kneels down in front of me. Laying his head on my thighs, he says, "It won't work. They'll have no trouble figuring out you had nothing to do with the business."

I drag my fingers through his dark hair, loving the feel of him there with me again. "I know. That was never the point. I just wanted to make it easier for your lawyer to argue it wasn't you."

Cash looks up at me and sighs. "It still won't work, and now everyone will know you lied. Doesn't that matter to you?"

Shaking my head, I laugh at that. "I don't care if people know I lied to some lady from the local news. Nobody will care anyway. The story of what I said to Shayla will be replaced by another more interesting one tomorrow. Somebody will give birth to eight babies or a turtle will be taught to run across a patio, and nobody will remember what I said. All that matters is I did all I could to help the man I love. Are you angry with me for that?"

He stands and pulls me up to my feet to wrap his arms around me. Against my cheek, he whispers, "I'm not angry. I'm just terrified you're going to get hurt again because of me."

I lean back and smile, hoping to see some happiness in his expression. "Well, at the very least, it got you to come see me. That's something."

"Savannah, I'd crawl on my hands and knees through shards of broken glass for miles to see you. Don't ever think I wouldn't give anything to be with you. That's the worst part of all of this after what it's done to the people I care about. What if I end up going to prison and I can't see you? I don't know how I'll live like that."

"Don't talk about it! You're not going anywhere. I'll take the blame for real then. It's not like they're going to put me in jail. I'm a wealthy white woman, and don't mention Martha Stewart," I say, hating how he's practically given up already on his future and ours.

"And if I have to, I'll go down to the Gainesville police station and remind them who my husband was and how much he supported this community. I'm a young widow and I've never used that even once to get sympathy. Maybe now's the time to start tugging on some heartstrings."

He stops my talking with a kiss that makes me go weak in the knees. When he pulls away, he presses a tiny kiss to my forehead and whispers against my skin, "I won't let you do that."

"Well, then you better stay next to me twenty-four seven because I will if I think they're going to take you away."

Sliding his hands up to my cheeks, he cradles my face and lets out a heavy sigh. "What am I going to do with you?"

"Whatever someone in love does."

Finally, he gives me a big smile that lights up his face and makes those beautiful blue eyes dance. "I do love you, Savannah."

"I know, and I love you. If I could do anything to make all of this disappear, I would, Cash. Giving some interview full of lies is the least I can do, I think. If there's anything else, name it and I'll do it."

Pulling me into his body, he hugs me tightly to him and kisses the top of my head. "I don't need you to do anything, Savannah. You loving me is more than I can ever ask for."

I press my cheek to the spot above his heart and smile as I feel it beat. He could ask for the moon and I'd do everything in my power to give it to him.

"I love you, Cash."

Now I just have to hope fate doesn't take this man away too.

CHAPTER SEVENTEEN

ash

THE MOMENT I STEP FOOT INTO MY APARTMENT, IT all comes back to me. All the days of thinking I had life by the tail. All the nights of enjoying expensive wine and sitting out on my balcony believing life would only get better from there.

I thought we were on the fast track to super success. Damon and I couldn't hire enough guys to handle the client requests. Money was rolling in. The idea that one day it would all come crashing down around us never occurred to me. I doubt it ever popped into his mind either.

Pulling out the phone I grabbed at the store on the way over here, I dial his number and head to the kitchen as it rings. One look in the refrigerator tells me eating isn't happening here today. I guess I better get some food if I don't want to starve.

Damon answers and warily says, "Hello?"

Instantly, I sense he's not okay, but then I remember he doesn't recognize this number. I'm damn lucky he bothered to answer at all.

"Damon, it's Cash. What's up?" I ask casually like I always did before everything happened.

The second he hears it's me, he changes to his usual self. "Dude, I've been wondering what's going on with you. My lawyer said not to call you, but I tried a few times. No go. What's going on?"

Walking out into the living room, I say, "My lawyer took my phone. He didn't want me to call anyone associated with the business. I pretty much blew that up the other night, so I figured I'd check in on you and see how you're doing."

He chuckles at my reference to calling Savannah. "Man, I have to know. What the fuck was that interview with that woman all about? You didn't bring someone in on our business without telling me, did you? My lawyer nearly shit a brick when he saw it. I didn't know what the hell it was about, so I just told him I was in the dark."

The interview. Jesus. I hadn't thought about that for three straight minutes.

"Yeah, that's Savannah. It's probably better if you don't know anything more than that, but no, I didn't cut her in on the business. She was trying to help. I'm not sure it's going to do anything like that, but if it hurts anyone, it will hurt her, not us."

Even as I say that, my chest tightens at the mere thought of the police giving her a hard time. She won't last fifteen minutes of them interrogating her. Savannah's not tough enough to deal with that.

"I didn't think so, but let me tell you, my lawyer was up one side of me and down the other after he watched it. I have to admit she did make some good points. I bet lots of people are wondering how we built the business from nothing since we are law school dropouts, like she said."

A sense of pride comes through loud and clear when he says that. He's right. People probably can't figure out how we did it. The truth is it happened one day at a time. Nobody bankrolled us. Nobody gave us some huge infusion of cash at the beginning. We just did it like most other people build businesses.

"We did a hell of a job, didn't we?" I say, sharing his pride.

"Damn, Cash. We did. What started out as helping that one girl with a date turned into a real moneymaker. Speaking of that, I hope you took care of yours the way you said you would."

Even now, we don't talk freely about the money. Old habits die hard, but it's better this way. Who knows what kind of surveillance, if any, the cops still have on us.

"Not to worry. I did what I said I would. You?"

Damon laughs. "You bet I did. My brother thinks they're never going to figure it out."

His older brother never fails to be even cockier than the two of us. It was Devon who egged him on to use cryptocurrency. Damon just wanted to use offshore accounts. That didn't seem like enough protection.

"Let's hope. I'd like to someday be able to do something with all of it."

"Yeah. I guess in the meantime we're just two law school dropouts. I'm staying at my parents' house after the cops turned over my apartment. Do you know they took the fucking TV? I couldn't stay there after that. What the hell did they want with the TV? Devon thinks they're under the impression that because it's a smart TV that it's like a computer. They can't be that fucking stupid, can they? Do they think I was sitting in my goddamned living room with a seventy inch monitor for my computer searching for restaurant menus and porn?"

The two of us laugh at how ludicrous that sounds. I can't imagine anyone would think that, but then again, I've heard stranger things.

"They made a mess of my apartment too, but I guess my regular size TV didn't impress them, so they left it. The place looked like it was robbed after they came through here," I say as I look around and see I still need to clean up more.

"Do you know all they could ask me was why I didn't have a laptop? Cash, I swear to God they thought I was like some Amish hustler or something," Damon says, laughing. "Over and over, they asked me about how the business worked and where my laptop was hidden, and every time I just shrugged. I think the one cop wanted to smack the shit out of me by the time it was over. As if anyone would need a goddamned laptop to do what we were doing."

That Damon is still so cocky makes me smile. If they send us both to prison, that'll change, but for now, it's nice to know something hasn't changed.

"I'm happy you're okay, man. Again, I would have called sooner, but my lawyer took my phone. It was like being transported back to when my parents were kids. I was thinking I needed to learn how to send smoke signals," I joke.

"They weren't going to find anything on that phone anyway, though, right?" he asks, suddenly sounding serious.

I quickly answer, not wanting to make him think I fucked up our plan. "No. The only people I ever contacted on that phone are you and a couple women."

"A couple women? Dude, are you sleeping with that interview chick? I thought you were still off and on with Emily."

Shaking my head at that terrible thought, I walk out onto my balcony to get some fresh air. "Her name is Savannah, and she and I started dating right before the shit hit the fan. And fuck that with Emily. The last time I saw her she was begging me to stay with her and then getting pissed and threatening me when I refused. I don't need that kind of crazy in my life. No thanks."

"You didn't tell her to say all of that in that interview, did you? Damn, man. I swear you're like the pied fucking piper. You can get women to do anything. I'm lucky if I can get Ashley to listen to me when I tell her to leave me alone."

"It isn't like that. Savannah was trying to help because she's worried about me. I never asked her to say a word. I wish she hadn't, to be honest. Now she's going to have to deal with the cops."

"Well, my lawyer says she's got enough money to hire some bigshot attorney who will probably drag the whole department through the mud if they go after her, so I wouldn't worry. I'm just hoping it helps us in some way."

I scan the horizon, still as impressed by my view as I was the day I first saw this apartment. Back then, Damon and I had big dreams to make a ton of money and have places ten times as incredible as this one. We made the money, but I never wanted to leave here once I moved in. You can buy a lot of things, but as I look out at the scene in front of me with the blue sky and city below, I know there are some things that turn out to be priceless.

"Hey, do you think Emily's the one who turned us in?" Damon asks, tearing me out of my thoughts.

Suddenly, I realize he might be right. "Damn. I don't know. Maybe. She was pissed the last time we talked. That was only a few days before it all went down, though. I feel like whatever sting operation they had going had to take more time than that, right?"

He takes a moment to think through my logic and answers, "Yes, I guess. My lawyer thinks it was some client who wasn't happy with the service."

"I can't imagine who. We had return customers

constantly. We weren't exactly not giving them what they want."

That makes Damon laugh louder than he has this entire phone call. "Dude, we gave those women just what they wanted. Well, not we. We just arranged it all. By the way, I have to say I was a little worried when I saw them dragging all those guys in for questioning. I thought one of them might know something, but my lawyer says the cops got nothing. You are all business, my friend, and that's why if we get out of this, I'm going to have to buy you a drink."

Smiling, I silently congratulate myself for a job well done. "I told you. No names on our end. Those guys got paid, and that's all that mattered to them. I just hope they don't get taken down for prostitution. You know, I hate that all the cops want to focus on is that. Like we were some pimps and the guys were hookers. This thing was so much more than that, and all they want to fixate on is the fucking sex."

"How much do you want to bet we had some of those cops' girlfriends and wives for clients, Cash? I'll bet you a hundred bucks we did."

I like that idea. It would be just desserts for people who can't see that the escort service was never about mere sex. Sure, we always assumed people were hooking up. Good for them. Everyone was a consenting adult, so why not?

But it wasn't just about fucking. Those women wanted something they couldn't find on their own or didn't have the time to find because they're busy. They wanted a man on their arm for events like Savannah's brother's wedding because their families and society make it next to impossible for a woman to attend events alone and not have to deal with a boatload of prying relatives with questions about their personal lives. Getting to show off a date for the night, even though he was a perfect stranger, gave them the freedom to enjoy themselves.

And if they got together after and had a good time? All the better. But the price never included that, and every one of our guys made sure to tell our clients that after I made sure they understood. So what if people got together and fucked?

Talk about a victimless crime.

"I better go, Cash. My mother has been making me eat three square meals a day since I came home, and it's time for one of them right now. I swear to God the next time you see me I'm going to be the size of a fucking house," he says with a chuckle.

"Better be careful. Ashley might not like the bigger and better Damon and could break up with you," I tease him.

"Bring on the food! If I had known that could work, I would have been gorging myself for months. Do you know she comes over here every night and we sit in the living room watching TV like we're in high school? She loves it too. I think getting fat is my last chance to freedom, man. Wish me luck."

"Good luck, Damon. Keep in touch and not just about this case."

"Will do. Gotta run. I think tonight is pot roast. See you, Cash!"

I stuff my phone back into my pocket and smile at the thought of Damon's always overbearing mother practically force feeding him this past week. She always was too hovering, and he used to hate that. Now, I guess it feels nice to know someone's looking out for him, even though he fucked up.

For a moment, I consider calling my mother. After today's talk with her, at least I know she'd answer the phone. Now's probably not a good idea, though. She and my Dad can use some time without me or my problems. I can call her tomorrow.

For tonight, all I want to do is relax for a little while, take a shower and get cleaned up, and then see Savannah. It's breaking Correlli's main rule for me, but I don't care anymore. The world knows she and I are together. If they didn't before today's interview, they do now.

All I care about is she's safe, and the best way for me to be sure of that is to have her by my side. It's certainly not the worst way for a man to spend his time.

CHAPTER EIGHTEEN

ash

As I walk into my bedroom wearing only a towel wrapped around my hips, I grab my replacement phone off my dresser and see Savannah texted me while I was in the shower.

Coming over in a little bit. I was thinking Chinese. Want anything in particular, or can it be ladies' choice? Let me know. Love you.

With a smile, I text back.

General Tso Chicken and an order of shrimp toast. Grab something to drink for us too. The fridge is pretty bare here after a week away.

A second later, Savannah sends back a message.

Will do. Alcohol or no? Actually, I'll bring both. See you soon! Love you.

We're like any other couple already. That's to be

expected, I guess. Except for the way we met and what's happened since that first date to her brother's wedding, it's been a perfectly normal relationship. Well, and my getting arrested and that stunt she pulled today.

Okay. Our relationship is definitely not like most people's.

I turn to walk over toward my closet to grab clothes to wear and stop. Grabbing my phone, I text her one last message.

Love you too.

Some strange sound out in the living room hits my ear, so I walk out to investigate. I don't have any windows open, so it's not possible that the wind pushed something over. A quick scan of the room tells me I must be hearing things, but then when I begin to walk back to the bedroom, I hear the sound again.

A quiet tapping noise. Is someone at my door?

Probably Savannah with her arms full with Chinese food for dinner.

I open the door and smile, but it's not her. Shaking my head, I frown, not in the mood to deal with Emily and her madness tonight.

Or any other time, actually.

"What do you want?" I ask, as rude as I can be.

She twirls her black hair around her forefinger and smiles. Dressed in a tiny shirt that barely covers her tits and a short skirt I'm sure shows off the goods if she moves too fast, she looks like she's ready for something I have no interest in.

"Did you know I was coming to see you, Cash? I used to like when you'd answer the door ready to go."

Confused for a split second, I look down and see I'm still only wearing a towel. Fuck. She doesn't need any encouragement, and now I'm standing here nearly naked in front of her.

"I just got out of the shower. I've got things to do tonight, so it's a bad time," I say as I move to close the door in her face.

She does what she always does and slithers underneath my arm to get inside. Christ, I don't want to have to deal with her right now.

Slamming the door shut, I march down the hallway to find her already making herself comfortable in the living room. I stop in front of where she's sitting on the couch and shake my head.

"No, Emily. You have to leave. I'm busy."

With those big doe eyes she puts on whenever she tries to convince someone to do what she wants and not what they want, she says with a pout, "Come on, Cash. You haven't been around for over a week after that whole getting arrested thing. You have to be horny, right?"

"Not really," I answer, staring down at her in disgust. "I got a solid pounding in jail, so I think I'm good for a while."

My crude joke makes her laugh, but still she doesn't budge. Reaching out to grab my towel, she giggles when I swat her hand away.

"Change teams on me, baby? One night in jail

doesn't usually do that to a man. You've seen the pics I put up on social media, but it's even better in person."

How I ever spent any time with this person baffles me as I stand here hating her now. What was I thinking then?

"I'm sure there's some adoring fan of yours who would love to get a look at the goods, Emily. Why don't you go find him or her and leave me alone?"

Again, she tries to grab my towel to take it off, but I step back so she can't reach me. Frustrated, she sulks and folds her arms across her chest.

"What's wrong with you, Cash? You know a nice fuck would take the edge off, and you have to be super stressed after all you've been through. Just having the news cameras following you for days drove you nuts, I bet. I know you, baby. You hate all that attention."

"Yeah, not an attention whore like some people. Now it's time for you to go. Get up or I'm going to pick you up and take you out like the trash."

She reluctantly stands up, but in a flash, she's pressed against me with her hands pawing at the towel knotted at my left hip. It easily comes undone, and I barely catch the towel before it falls to the floor leaving me buck naked in front of her.

"Enough, Emily! Fucking go! I don't want you. I told you that last time, and I've been telling you that with every word I've uttered since I opened the door and saw you standing there. Go and find someone else who wants what you have going on. I'm not interested."

"I don't believe that," she says with a pout that's

clearly something she's putting on for show. "You and I love each other, Cash. If I didn't love you, would I have come over here every night once I found out the cops took you away?"

"You only love yourself, Emily. It's all about you. What a man can do for you. What a man can tell you to make you feel beautiful. I'm not that guy. I don't have any money anymore. You have to realize that. So go and find somebody else."

As I turn my back to wrap the towel around me again, she slides her hands around my body and grabs my cock. "I can get you hard in a second, baby, and we can get busy like we used to. If my hand won't do it, my mouth definitely can. I'm not wearing any underwear, so you can just bend me over the back of the couch like you love doing and give it to me. I've missed you, Cash. Let me show you how much."

Fuck, this woman won't give up. How many times does she have to hear no before it sinks into her sad little head?

Spinning around, I push her away. She falls back onto the couch, but instead of looking upset or hurt, she takes this as a sign that it's go time.

Emily lifts her skirt to reveal she didn't lie about not wearing anything underneath. Legs spread wide open, she gives me a bird's eye view of her perfectly smooth pussy. My cock should be doing something at this moment. I mean, what guy doesn't get excited seeing that, even if he doesn't plan to fuck the woman? It's there for the taking, but more than that, it's a pussy.

But I feel nothing. I look at her, lifting my gaze to meet hers as she waits eagerly to hear me say I give in and then a second later bury my cock inside her for some angry sex, the only kind we've ever had, and shake my head.

"Sorry. Not in the mood. Pull your skirt down. You look desperate."

Still, she won't give up. With her skirt up around her waist, she pushes her foot out to try to stroke my cock with her toes. I move back so she can't touch me and laugh. Emily is definitely persistent. I'll give her that, even if I won't give her anything else.

"No! We belong together, Cash March. You know it, and I know it. Stop trying to pretend you don't want me."

"I don't. Now go, or I swear to God, I'm going to toss you out into the hallway."

She doesn't move a muscle for a long moment as I glare down at her hoping she'll finally figure out I mean business. I've been pretty blunt. How she couldn't understand basic English escapes me, but Emily has never been very bright.

Finally, she angrily tugs her skirt down and stands up. Her eyes narrow, and she points at me so her finger almost touches my shoulder.

"You have no idea how many people love me, Cash. Whenever I post pics of me, no matter what I'm wearing, I get hundreds and hundreds of likes. Sometimes even thousands. You don't know what you're giving up with me."

With every word, I move from hating her to

pitying her. She exists only in other people's eyes, and now that I don't care, she can't handle that to me, she doesn't exist anymore. That's all we ever were together.

Emily and the man whose one and only job was to be her mirror.

"Go home, or go anywhere you like. I don't care. We aren't anything to each other anymore," I say as I pull her toward the door.

Just before I get her out of the apartment, she turns and kisses me hard, catching me off guard. She thrusts her hands under the towel and grabs my cock as she forces her tongue into my mouth like some pushy prom date. I shake my head to be rid of her and push her away even harder this time, making her slam into the wall across from me.

She stares up at me with a stunned look for a few moments, but when that fades away, all I get is anger. "Now I'm happy I helped the cops with that stupid business of yours," she says, nearly spitting the words out of her mouth. "Yeah, I was the one who told them all about everything. I hope you spend the rest of your life in jail, Cash March! You just lost the best thing you ever had."

Damon was right. She did rat us out. Bitch.

I open my mouth to tell her to never fucking come here again, but the front door opens and Savannah walks in. I move to stop her so she doesn't see Emily, but when I do, the towel finally drops, leaving me standing there naked in front of her and another woman.

She looks at me with pure hurt in her eyes and shakes her head while I crouch down to get that goddamned towel that can't seem to stay on my body tonight. "What's going on here?"

Before I can answer her truthfully and explain nothing happened, Emily points at her and snaps, "Who the fuck is this?"

I can't decide if I want to throw her out first or try to make Savannah understand this isn't what it looks like. For a few seconds, the three of us stare at each other like none of us know what to do next.

And then Savannah steps toward me, hands me the bag from the Chinese restaurant and a bottle of soda she's been holding, and turns to stand toe to toe with Emily. About the same height, she squares her shoulders and looks her directly in the eye.

"I'm his girlfriend, and you know what? It's time for you to go. Now either walk out on your own or I'll remove you from this apartment, but either way, you're leaving."

Emily doesn't budge, her mouth hanging open in shock, and when she doesn't move, Savannah lives up to her word and pushes her out the door. Then she slams it shut, locks it, and turns around to face me as I stand there in utter amazement.

"Should I have asked her name before throwing her out? That seems kind of rude of me not to now that I think of it."

Leaning down, I kiss her beautiful mouth and smile. "No need. Her name is Emily, but she won't be an issue anymore."

Savannah gives me a big smile and takes the bag of Chinese food out of my arms. "Good. Are you ready to eat?"

"Sure, but you don't want to hear my explanation for all of that? Nothing happened. I swear."

She shrugs and begins walking toward the kitchen. "I believe you. I'm starving. I didn't get anything alcoholic to drink, though, so if you were expecting that, I'm sorry to say you're going to be disappointed."

I follow and catch up with her as she begins to unpack our dinner from the brown paper bag onto the counter. She doesn't look upset, but my experience with women tells me finding the man she loves in a compromising position likely upset her. On top of everything else she's had to deal with being with me, I wouldn't blame her if she was downright pissed.

"Hey, maybe we should talk?" I say as I set the bottle of soda down next to my General Tso chicken dinner.

Turning to face me, she nods. "Okay. What's up?"

"I mean about what just happened. Nothing happened, not with Emily, I mean, but I'd understand if you weren't happy. You know, walking in and seeing that certainly couldn't have been great."

Savannah nods again and then stands on her tiptoes to kiss me sweetly on the lips. "You could say that, but I did a quick assessment of the situation and decided everything was okay. She had to go, of course, but you weren't guilty of doing anything wrong."

"A quick assessment?" I ask, wondering why she suddenly sounds like some SEAL team commando.

Looking up at me with innocence in her eyes, she explains, "Your penis was hanging out, Cash, so my attention was naturally drawn to that. Since it was soft and it didn't look like it had been anywhere that would make it wet, I concluded that you didn't have sex with her. After that, I read your body language and decided you weren't happy with her being here. Since you're a gentleman, you probably didn't tell her to get the hell out, so I took matters into my own hands. I think they gave you white rice instead of fried rice, so if you want to switch with me, that's okay."

I want to say half a dozen things in response to that explanation, but suddenly my brain seems devoid of any thought but how incredible she is. When she turns to continue unpacking the bag, I move behind her and slide my arms around her waist.

Setting my chin on her shoulder, I whisper, "You are the most wonderful woman in the world, Savannah Gardener. Do you know that?"

She turns her head and gives me a tiny peck. "Thank you. So any decision on the rice issue? I think I must have messed up when I was ordering because I don't think I've ever had any Chinese restaurant screw up an order."

I nuzzle her neck, loving how the sweetness of her skin fills my nose. "Whichever you like. I'm not a huge rice eater anyway. I think I'm going to go get dressed, so I'll be right back."

That makes her spin around in my hold, shaking her head. "No way. Stay in the towel. I have plans for what I want for dessert."

"Not fortune cookies? Don't you want to know what the future holds?"

Her gaze drifts down my body to where my cock pushes against the towel. Smiling, she says, "I can predict the future, actually. I can say, without a shadow of a doubt, that dessert is going to be your favorite part of the meal."

I cup my hand over the front of the towel and smile. "I don't doubt it."

Then she skims her fingertips along the skin between my hips and adds, "In fact, I think tonight calls for having dessert first."

CHAPTER NINETEEN

avannah

I CROUCH DOWN IN FRONT OF CASH AND PRESS MY lower back up against his kitchen cabinets to keep my balance. Going down on him before dinner hadn't been my original plan, but things change.

He just looks too damn good standing there in that towel for me to let that go to waste.

Tugging the towel off his hips, I slide my hand around his hard cock and smile up at him. "Sure you're not hungry and I should wait?"

Cash shakes his head as a smile lifts the corners of his mouth. "I could be a starving man who hasn't eaten in weeks and I'd still want this from you before anything else."

Giggling, I stroke him slowly. "That does not sound healthy."

He stuffs his hands into my hair and tugs my head forward until the head of his cock presses against my lips. I sort of want to tease him a little more, but our dinner is getting cold and I really was looking forward to shrimp with lobster sauce, so it's probably a good idea if I take care of business.

I open my mouth and slowly slide him over my lips, loving the feel of his silky soft skin. He tastes masculine and musky, even though he just had a shower. If I was insecure, I might think that's because he had a girl here for God only knows how long before I arrived, but I'm not.

He's already shown me the kind of man he is. I'm not worried he's a cheater.

Above me, Cash moans when the tip of his cock bumps up against the back of my throat. I flick my tongue along his balls and hum against his skin to drive him crazy. The vibration hits him hard, and he pushes his hips forward so I can't do anything but deep throat him.

Knowing that, I swallow hard and watch his eyes open wide in excitement. I may look sweet and innocent, but I have some experience pleasing a man.

"Oh, fuck…this isn't going to take long, Savannah, if you keep doing things like that."

He sounds disappointed, and although I don't usually mind a long sex session, I can smell my food behind me on the counter just waiting to be eaten. So I begin bobbing my head up and down, taking him all the way down to the base and then back up until the head is the only thing still in my mouth. Sucking hard, I give it a little lick with the tip of my tongue and take all of him again, over and over as he moans loudly above me and pulls hard on my hair.

It only takes a few minutes, just like he warned, before he's fucking my mouth like a man desperate to come. I hold onto his hips, sinking my fingertips into his skin, and with each thrust, I moan around his cock and revel in the grunts he makes. He tightens his hold on my hair even more, practically pulling it out by the roots, but I'm so excited by this that I can barely feel the pain as it dances across my scalp.

With one last push of his hips, he buries his cock in my mouth and I feel him come against my tongue. He holds my head tightly against him, filling my nose with the masculine scent that's so him. My eyes closed, I swallow every drop he gives, and when he leans back and his cock slides out of my mouth, I look up to see a very satisfied Cash.

"Damn, that was some dessert."

With a smile, I stand up and kiss him. "That's for being a good boy. Now it's time for dinner."

I turn to get our food, but he pulls me to him and kisses me long and deep. I melt into his arms, loving how it feels to have them around me.

"I love you, Savannah, and not just because you do things like that."

"So if I never went down on you again, you'd be okay?" I ask with a giggle, knowing the answer before he even gives it to me.

A look of disappointment crosses his face. "Well, not okay, but I'd still love you."

I tap the tip of his nose and smile. "Don't worry. I like doing that for you. It gets me all hot. Right now, though, I'm starving, so if you have any special dessert for me, I hope you're okay with me getting it at the usual dessert time."

"Trust me. I have something for you for dessert. I'm thinking whipped cream with it too."

I'm not sure if he has a treat for me that I can actually eat or he's talking about spraying whipped cream all over my body and eating that himself as he goes down on me. Either way, I'll love it.

Just like I love him.

CASH LEANS BACK AGAINST THE COUCH CUSHION and closes his eyes. "I think I have food coma. Did they give you an extra-large order of General Tso? I haven't exactly been starving while I've been at my brother's, but I'm stuffed."

"No, just the regular size," I say as I snuggle up next to him. "I think it might be all the rice you ate. For a guy who isn't a big rice eater, you gobbled down nearly a whole pint of the stuff."

He opens his eyes and smiles. "I guess I need to revise my position on rice. Just give me a minute and then I'm going to give you your dessert."

"It's not food, is it?" I ask, suddenly worried I might actually have to consume more after that feast we just finished.

My question makes him laugh. "No. The only

edible food I have in this apartment walked through the door with you."

"Oh, okay. Because if it was something like a real dessert, I might have to give it a little while because I'm stuffed too."

He pulls me to him and closes his eyes. "Just a few minutes. I promise."

One heavy sigh and a minute later, he's asleep. After all he's been through for the past week, I can't blame him.

I lay my head on his chest and close my eyes while I think about how much I miss him every time he's gone from my side. It's all happened so quickly, but that doesn't mean anything. When you know how you feel about someone, time and how long you've known them becomes unimportant.

All that matters is he loves me and I love him. Everything else we'll handle.

WHEN I OPEN MY EYES, I LOOK DOWN MY BODY TO see Cash kissing the insides of my thighs. It must be dessert time.

"I woke up just at just the right time."

He smiles against my leg and winks. "I like to think I have enough skill at this that you wouldn't sleep through it."

As I start to joke that you never know since I tend to sleep like the dead, his thumb brushes between my legs and begins drawing tight circles on my clit.

Suddenly, my ability to speak vanishes, that area of my brain completely overrun by pure pleasure.

"I like that you started to say something and then as soon as I touched you, nothing. Tells me I hit the right spot," he says as he kisses where my left leg meets my body.

His warm breath drifts over my exposed skin, thrilling me while I wait to feel his mouth on me. The anticipation is sweet torture, with every second that ticks by making me want this more and more.

I lift my hips off the couch to give him a not-so-subtle hint that it's time for dessert to start, and he looks up at me with pure mischief in his blue eyes. He has no idea the effect he has on me just with a glance.

"I'd like you to touch that spot again, but this time with your mouth, please," I say sweetly.

He doesn't wait another moment before pressing his mouth to my needy clit and giving it a gentle suck. My eyes roll back in my head as pleasure rolls through me with every flick of his tongue. I'm a slave to that mouth of his.

I don't know how long he teases me, taking me to the edge of an orgasm and then easing me back, but I finally can't wait any longer and stuff my hand against the back of his head. He looks up, seemingly confused like he doesn't understand what could be the urgency, but then he smiles.

"Anything you'd like?" he asks and then licks the full length of my pussy until he stops right below my clit.

"Yes! I'd like to come, but you won't let me. All this teasing is very frustrating, Cash."

"Then I better do something about it."

Before I can say I think he should, his mouth closes around my clit and he slides two fingers inside me. Fireworks go off behind my eyes as my release tears through me after waiting so long for just this exquisite feeling.

"Yes! Don't stop..." I whimper, desperate to have this continue until I can't bear it any longer.

His tongue laps at me while his fingers fuck me, curling just right to graze that one spot inside that makes an orgasm better than any feeling in the world. And then, I feel a second one hit me and buck against his face with abandon, my body craving every single touch of his tongue and mouth I can have on me.

When he sits back on his heels, I collapse into the cushions and sigh, more content than I ever remember being. "That dessert was fantastic. I'd like to have that delivered to me for after every meal."

"Glad you liked it. It's a Cash March specialty."

My brain feels fuzzy, like I lost oxygen when I came and now I can't think straight. Even more, I think I want to sleep again.

Closing my eyes, I whisper, "I love you."

I feel his lips touch mine and he says, "I love you, Savannah. You look like you're going to pass out."

"Just for a second or two. I think you have the honor of being the only man I've ever met who could affect me like this."

As I drift off, he kisses me again and whispers, "Good. I want to be the only man who affects you at all in any way."

CHAPTER TWENTY

ash

THREE MONTHS LATER

Savannah tightens her hold on my hand as we walk up toward the front door to my grandmother's house. It's a beautiful, sunny day and she looks stunning in a red long sleeved dress with a white bow that crosses just under her ribs, like my perfect Christmas present.

And the perfect woman to introduce to my family.

She stops about two steps away from the porch and turns to look at me. "Are you sure this is a good idea? I'm dying to meet everyone, but it's the holidays, Cash. Christmas was just two days ago. This seems like the time for all of you to be together, not having some new person put in the mix."

I lean down and kiss her on her red lips tinted to

match her dress. "You're not some new person. You're the woman I've lived with for the past two months. I want everyone to meet you and see how lucky I am. What better time than at the holidays, especially since you look like my Christmas present?"

My joke doesn't go over as well as I would like, and her frown deepens. "This isn't funny, Cash. I'm nervous. I didn't care if anyone thought I was a liar when I did that interview, but that was people I knew. These are people in your family. What if they don't see that I did that because I love you?"

"They will. Trust me. I know they will. They already do. My mother said when she saw you on TV that day that she would want to meet any woman who loved her son that much to do what you did. Well, today she gets to meet you. It's been a little over three months since we started dating. It's time."

When she doesn't smile, I add, "Because if I don't introduce you to them now, they're going to think I made you up, like you're just an imaginary girlfriend instead of the real life, flesh and blood woman I adore."

"Don't try to joke your way out of this," she mumbles.

I love how cute she's being about my family meeting her. As if my dating a woman who's this gorgeous and as wealthy as she is would ever be a problem. She acts as if she's some girl I picked up on the way over instead of the beautiful woman I one day intend on marrying.

Not that she knows about that last part yet.

"Ready?"

Savannah runs her hands over her long brown hair and takes a deep breath in. "Do I look okay? Red sometimes leaves me all washed out, and even though I thought I looked good this morning at the house, now I'm feeling like being around all this water is making me look pale."

Cradling her face in my hands, I kiss her as the last word leaves her mouth. "You look perfect. Trust me, they're going to love you."

She looks up at me and lets her breath out slowly. Suddenly, her eyes open wide in pure terror. "I think I forgot everyone's name! Run through them all again, please."

I can't help but laugh at how she's so nervous about meeting the March and Jackson clan. Maybe I should have told her more embarrassing stories about all of us so she'd know there's no reason to worry.

"Okay, here goes. My grandmother's name is Alexandria. She's who my brother is named after. My parents are Cassian and Olivia."

Rolling her eyes, she pushes my shoulder. "I know the immediate family, Cash. It's the extended one I'm mixing up."

"Got it. Well, the brother who looks like my father and me is Kane. The one who looks like Alex is Stefan. Liam is the tall guy around our age who looks like me, and Cade is the one who looks like Alex."

She nods as I speak, looking more enthusiastic with each second. "Okay. I think I got it. Stefan and Cade are father and son and look like Alex with that side of the family's dark hair and brown eyes. There's a sister in there too, right?"

"Yeah. Ava, and she looks like her mother, who is Stefan's wife. Remember her name?"

Suddenly, fear fills Savannah's eyes again. "No! Wait, is it Abbi?"

"No. She's the blond who's married to Kane. Remember, blond with the guy who looks like me and my father, and brunettes are related to Stefan with the brown hair and brown eyes."

"Okay, okay. I think I have it. But what if the brunettes are standing with the uncle who looks like you? I'm going to get confused."

She has no idea of the history of that topic, so I just shake my head and smile. "That won't happen. The brunettes are never alone with Kane."

"That's a very weird statement. You know that, right?"

I take her hand and begin walking toward my grandmother's front door. "Not if you know the stories."

"So what? Does that mean the blond, Abbi, is never going to be standing just with Stefan?" she asks.

It's a logical question, but since little of what happens with my family is logical, I don't have a good answer for her. "She might, but that's not an issue. Oh, and don't forget there's Wilder. He sort of looks like me with dark hair and blue eyes, but he's always miserable at these things. He's Kane and Abbi's son."

Waving her hands excitedly, she says, "Oh, and he's never next to Cade because they hate each other."

"Right. Cade will probably have his girlfriend Hailey with him, which will mean there won't be any angry fights between those two. Without her here, things between Cade and Wilder might get ugly."

As I ring the doorbell, Savannah says under her breath, "And Olivia has the red hair, which makes her unique amongst everyone in the family."

I smile and nod my head. "Exactly."

ON MY WAY OUT OF THE HOUSE, ALEX CATCHES ME on the porch and pulls me aside. Curious if I missed something big while I was getting Savannah another glass of wine, I glance around and see everyone looks the same as they did ten minutes ago. Nobody is bloody, and it seems like everyone's still talking to each other.

"What's up? Did something happen?"

He laughs, probably because I sound paranoid. I do sound overly worried, but I've seen this family's get-togethers devolve into drunken melees before.

"No. I just thought you should give Savannah some time with Mom and Grandma. The three of them are down at the table talking, and this is the first time she's been left alone with them. Something up, or are you just a helicopter boyfriend now?"

I shrug and look over at them laughing at something my grandmother is saying. "No, and I'm not a helicopter boyfriend. She was just nervous about meeting everyone today, so I wanted her to know I'm right here with her."

"What's she nervous about?" he asks, likely as confused as I am about why she thought everyone here wouldn't love her.

"I don't know. I guess it could be because her family is a little fucked up. Her sister Cheyenne is cool, but the rest of them are a nightmare."

"And we're not fucked up? Look at Wilder over there a hundred feet away from everyone else. Anyone watching this party from the outside would think he's some stranger we dragged in off the street. Any minute now, Abbi will walk over with a soda, like she does at every one of these, and he'll tell her he's fine. Then he'll sulk for the rest of the time before he disappears."

I shrug since that's nothing new. "Well, that's Wilder. I did sort of try to explain the whole way Shay is never alone with Kane, but Abbi can be alone with Stefan. It would have been too hard to get into all the details, though, so I just dropped it. Maybe on the ride home, I'll explain it to Savannah now that she's met everyone."

Alex slaps me on the back and chuckles. "You have to love this family, don't you? Well, I won't keep you from your landing pad, Helicopter Cash. I guess I'll go hang out with the single guys left, which means Liam since Wilder isn't anyone I want to spend time with today or any other day."

Tilting Savannah's wine glass up to my mouth, I take a drink. "Don't count on it. I think he's with that girl he's working with. He mentioned something about it before when we were all talking, remember?"

My brother's face twists into a look of horror. "Are you telling me that only leaves Wilder? No thanks."

I begin to walk down the steps toward where Savannah sits with my mother and grandmother and look back at Alex. "Maybe it's time you started bringing someone to these things so you aren't stuck alone or talking to Wilder."

A sly smile lights up his face. "Not quite yet, big brother. But maybe there's a service that could get me a date for the day? Know anything like that?"

Fucking bust ass. Leave it to him to bring that up.

I hand Savannah her wine glass and sit down on the bench next to her as she listens to my mother tell the story of when I was small and decided I wanted to learn to throw the javelin so I could compete in the Olympics. It's a humiliating story full of details like how I threw a stick into the china cabinet in the dining room and shattered the glass and how I nearly poked my eye out before giving up on my Summer Olympics dream.

"Alex stopped me and I took a drink, just in case you're wondering why it's not full," I whisper in her ear while my mother regales her with my failed track and field attempts.

"So, thankfully, he gave that up before he lost an eye and I lost my fine china. He was a good boy, though. Just had some odd ideas about what he wanted to do when he grew up."

Savannah turns to look at me and smiles. "You sound like you were adorable."

"He was," my grandmother says and reaches across the table to touch her hand. "I have pictures inside. Come in and we'll look through all of them."

Before I can stop that nightmare from coming true, Savannah leans over and kisses me. "I'll be back in a little bit. I can't wait to see these pictures!"

I want to catch her before she walks away, but my mother stops with a shake of her head. "Let your grandmother have her fun. You don't have to worry. It's just that shrine she keeps of all your pictures and awards and achievements. It's not like she's going to show her anything unflattering."

As much as that might be true, I still don't love the idea of her alone with my grandmother for any extended period of time. Alexandria March has a way of making things happen that people don't even realize before it's done.

"I guess. So what do you think?" I ask, suddenly as nervous as Savannah was before we walked into the house hours ago.

My mother smiles and tilts her head slightly to the side. "She's as beautiful as she was that day on the TV, Cash. What's not to like about her?"

I cringe at her mention of the interview. "You didn't bring that day up, did you? She was afraid you'd hold it against her and not like her because of it."

"Oh, honey. How could I hold that against her? She did that because she loves you. It didn't make everything better, but she risked the police looking at her for a crime all for you."

"No, it didn't fix things, but everything's going to be okay soon now that they've dropped everything but the one charge."

I don't say what that charge is, even though my mother knows what it is. Talking about having to plead guilty to a prostitution charge and pay a fine is bad enough, but I don't want to talk about it on the day I've brought the woman I love to meet my family.

My mother's cheeks turn red from the blush she gets whenever we talk about all that happened. I guess it's not surprising. To her, I'll always be that little boy throwing sticks in the yard. Thinking of me as a man running an escort service or sleeping with a woman, even Savannah, isn't something she's ever going to be comfortable with.

"Where's Savannah?" my father asks before sitting down next to my mother.

"In the house with your mother. She's showing Savannah pictures of Cash from the shrine," my mother says with a smile.

"I'm wondering if I should dread it now or wait until she comes back and tells me stories I've tried to forget," I mumble before taking a gulp of wine.

My father throws his head back and laughs. He knows his mother all too well to know that very well may happen.

"I wouldn't worry. It's a shrine. It's not like she kept the bad stuff to show off. Sort of goes against the concept of a shrine."

My mother nudges his shoulder. "That's what I told him. Alexandria only shows off the best stuff. She'll have Savannah thinking our son is the second coming by the time she's done in there."

That doesn't sound bad at all. Considering I'm an unemployed guy hoping to find a job after everything settles down with the case, and I'll have a criminal record, even if it is only a misdemeanor, having someone say I'm a good guy would be nice.

"She's really sweet, just like you said she was, Cash. Your mother and I like her a lot."

Relief washes over me at hearing they, like Alex, think Savannah's as wonderful as I do. "Thanks, Dad. I'm crazy about her."

He gives me a big smile. "I can tell. Anyone with eyes could, I bet."

My mother leans over and wraps her arms around him. "What did you give her for Christmas?"

The way she asks that sounds strange, and the look in her eyes tells me she's up to something. "I'm taking her away for a weekend skiing around New Year's. Why?"

"Well, I looked at her left hand and didn't see anything. I was just wondering if that's coming soon."

Mystery solved.

My parents sit across from me waiting for my answer, the two of them staring at me like I'm about to announce big news, but I'm not ready to let them in on my secret just yet. It's not time, and I need to ask Savannah first before anyone else knows.

So I play it as cool and casual as I can. That way, they'll be surprised when I pop the question too.

"We've only been together for a few months. Maybe in time. We'll see."

The two of them seem to deflate right in front of my eyes. Who knew my parents were so eager to see me get married?

"And I'm not exactly in a position to do anything, remember. I don't even have a job, and until this case gets wrapped up, I'm still dealing with legal issues. Savannah deserves to be asked by someone who deserves her. I'm not there yet."

Sadness creeps into my mother's eyes, but my father shakes his head. "Don't ever think that way, Cash. You're a good man. This family has its fair share of rogues and rebels. To be honest, I'm not even sure you rank in the top five."

Considering the stories I've heard of his father, Kane, Stefan, and him back in the day, he might be right.

Behind me, I hear Savannah and my grandmother coming toward the table, and I turn around to see the woman I love holding the eight by ten gold framed version of my fourth grade school picture. The ugliest school picture out of all twelve I had taken. The one where my hair had a cowlick and my mother decided that was the perfect day to dress me in a tan and yellow striped sweater.

So much for the beloved shrine.

"Cash, your grandmother has the most wonderful bunch of pictures of you throughout your life. She says there's a funny story that goes with this one, so I thought I'd bring it out and ask you to tell me."

My father bursts into laughter, barely able to get the words out as he asks, "Funnier than the picture itself?"

I look over at my mother for some help, but it's all she can do to hide her own laughter as she buries her face in his shoulder. Nothing like being humiliated by your own family when you finally bring your girlfriend around to meet them.

Savannah sits down and kisses me as my parents laugh and tell the story everyone thinks is hysterical about how I woke up late that morning, my mother dressed me like some deranged Waldo, and then we couldn't get my hair to lay right before I had to run to catch the bus so I wouldn't miss school. This rogue sounds pretty damn lame right now.

While everyone talks and has a good time, she leans over and whispers in my ear, "I love you, no matter what you looked like in fourth grade. Don't be upset. I had such a good time hearing about what a great kid you were. When she suggested I bring this out, I didn't want to offend her, so I said yes. But I think it's adorable, even if your hair is doing that weird flippy thing in the front."

"Thankfully, I got better with age."

She nods and looks over at me parents still having a good time reliving that day. "Things look like they only get better from here too."

As my mother tickles my father and he laughs that way that sounds like it's coming from deep inside him,

I have to admit I hope someday I'll have a life like they do. Cassian March III and Olivia Lucas gave me everything I could possibly want in this world, including a great example of how to love someone.

Now it's my turn to take what I know and make a life of my own with the woman of my dreams. I can only hope in twenty years when I'm sitting around with my kids that they look at Savannah and me and think we lived a life they could be proud of.

We started out a little rough, and I'll forever be guilty of a crime, but between the two of us, we have enough love to make it. And we have a family around us to help us remember even when things get rocky, there's always people who love you for who you are.

LOOK FOR FLIRTATIOUS, THE FIRST BOOK IN LIAM JACKSON'S DUET, COMING SOON!

ABOUT THE AUTHOR

K.M. Scott writes contemporary romance stories of sexy, intense, and unforgettable love. A New York Times and USA Today bestselling author, she's been in love with romance since reading her first romance novel in junior high (she was a very curious girl!). Under her Gabrielle Bisset name, she write paranormal and historical romance. She lives in Pennsylvania with a herd of animals and when she's not writing can be found reading or feeding her TV addiction.

Be sure to visit K.M.'s Facebook page at **https://www.facebook.com/kmscottauthor** for all the latest on her books, along with giveaways and other goodies! And to hear all the news on K.M. Scott books first, sign up for her newsletter today and be sure to visit her website at **http://www.kmscottbooks.com**

BOOKS BY K.M. SCOTT:

Crash Into Me (Heart of Stone #1)

Fall Into Me (Heart of Stone #2)

Give In To Me (Heart of Stone #3)

Heart of Stone Volume One

Ever After (Heart of Stone #4)

A Heart of Stone Christmas (Heart of Stone #5)

Return To Me (Heart of Stone #6)

Forever With Me (Heart of Stone #7)

Heart of Stone Volume Two

Hard As Stone (Heart of Stone #8)

Set In Stone (Heart of Stone #9)

Silent As A Stone (Heart of Stone #10)

Heart of Stone Volume Three

All of Me (Heart of Stone #11)

Temptation (Club X #1)

Surrender (Club X #2)

Possession (Club X #3)

Satisfaction (Club X #4)

Acceptance (Club X #5)

Complete Club X Series Box Set

Notorious (NeXt #1)

Infamous (NeXt #2)

Ravenous (NeXt #3)

Ambitious (NeXt #4)

If I Dream (Corrupted Love #1)

If You Fight (Corrupted Love #2)

If We Fall (Corrupted Love #3)

Corrupted Love Trilogy Box Set

Crave (Addicted To You #1)

Adore (Addicted To You #2)

Shatter (Addicted To You #3)

Claim (Addicted To You #4)

Addicted To You Series Box Set

In The Darkness (Project Artemis #1)

After The Storm (Project Artemis #2)

Behind The Scenes (Project Artemis #3)

Project Artemis Box Set

Hard Work (Finding The One #1)

Big Love (Finding The One #2)

Sweet Things

Private Secretary

K.M.'S BOOKS ARE IN AUDIOBOOK TOO!

BOOKS BY K.M. SCOTT WRITING AS
GABRIELLE BISSET:

Vampire Dreams Revamped (A Sons of Navarus Prequel)

Blood Avenged (Sons of Navarus #1)

Blood Betrayed (Sons of Navarus #2)

Longing (A Sons of Navarus Short Story)

Blood Spirit (Sons of Navarus #3)

The Deepest Cut (A Sons of Navarus Short Story)

Blood Prophecy (Sons of Navarus #4)

Blood Craving (Sons of Navarus #5)

Blood Eclipse (Sons of Navarus #6)

Blood Ascendant (Sons of Navarus #7)

The Sons of Navarus Box Set #1

The Sons of Navarus Box Set #2

Stolen Destiny (Destined Ones Duet #1)

Destiny Redeemed (Destined Ones Duet #2)

Love's Master

Masquerade

The Victorian Erotic Romance Trilogy